Alianne Donnelly

To Beau —

With gratitude for the lovely pen with which I sign my name. I plan to use it often and for a very long time!

Love,
Aly D.

The Beast Series
Special Collector's Edition

This is a work of fiction. The characters, incidents and dialogues in this book are of the author's imagination and are not to be construed as real. Any resemblance to actual events or persons, living or dead, is completely coincidental.

Copyright © 2013 by Alianne Donnelly

All rights reserved. No part of this publication may be reproduced, stored in a retrieval system, or transmitted in any form or by any means, digital, electronic, mechanical, photocopying, recording, or otherwise, or conveyed via the Internet or a Web site without prior written permission of the author.

ISBN-13: 978-14-9354-326-7 (print)
ISBN-10:   14-9354-326-1 (print)

Originally published as two eBooks by Alianne Donnelly, Smashwords 2012: 9781476446370 (*Bastien*)
9781465921581 (*The Beast*)

Foreword

Dear reader,

When I began this tale, it was nothing more than impromptu chapters of a strange little retelling of the classic *Beauty and the Beast*, posted on my blog at sort of regular intervals just for the fun of it. Back then I had no idea it would be anything more than that. I suppose I should have known better.

I had just I made the whole of it available as a freebie when Bastien showed up in my head and refused to leave until I told his side of the story. So I did. But I was no longer going to be satisfied with simply posting the chapters on some website. No, *Bastien* demanded the royal treatment with editing, formatting, fancy cover page, and all. Have you ever tried arguing with a spoiled rotten prince? I wouldn't recommend it.

Obviously, he got what he wanted. Damn his handsome hide…

What you are holding in your hands is a special collector's edition of this story's two separate novellas, originally published as eBooks in 2012. As the prequel, *Bastien* comes first so you can have a front row seat to his wicked fall from humanity. This isn't your typical fairy tale. It's dark and ugly, and Bastien himself is not exactly a poster boy for Prince Charming. Believe me when I say he very much deserved his punishment. And though I am fully aware that he is a royal bastard—a title he very much likes and takes every opportunity to demonstrate—there were times while writing his side of the story when his tough face slipped just a little and I could steal small glimpses into his heart. That side of him ended up claiming a piece of my heart in return.

In the second half of this book you will find the original novella which takes place several months after *Bastien*. In order to remain true to the spirit of *The Beast*, the story is included here in its minimally edited format. Most of it is exactly as it was first posted on my blog: somewhat rough around the edges, just like the Beast himself. But now it has a new ending, completely rewritten from the original. It is a great deal richer and gives a much more satisfying closure to this tale.

We each have that one fairy tale which resonates with us on some deeper level. This is mine. The story of Beauty and her Beast has always been very dear to me. It has at its core values which can easily become lost in the shuffle of everyday life: love, family, integrity, bravery, loyalty, and trust. I wrote this to remind myself of each and every one of them, plus one more: magic.

I think everyone should have a little of that in their life, don't you?

Happy reading!

~ Alianne

Bastien

Chapter One

My earliest memory is of my nurse dipping a curtsy and calling me "my Lord Bastien." It was on the day of my fourth birthday, the day my parents' bodies were brought in from the cold. That year the winter was so frigid the gardeners couldn't break ground to bury them. My noble parents were laid on a slab of stone in the ice room, side by side as though asleep, to wait for spring.

Frost preserved them quite well for a while. I would go to them each day to wish them a good morning and pretend they answered the same. "Good morning, Bastien. Another day has dawned. Another day in which you are Lord of all you see." When the thaw came, they were gone. Only an engraved stone marker remained deep in the garden, set so far back I could not see it from my room.

I am Lord Bastien Sauvage III, Duke of Colline, second cousin to King Arnaud. A prince of this kingdom. It's a delicious mouthful. So am I. My castle stands proud near the village of Fauve, surrounded by forests and fields. Game is plentiful here and the earth fertile. None in my demesne go hungry, least of all me.

Tonight I stare out into the velvet black, watching the moon make its way across the sky. It is summer, the feeble breeze bringing with it more warmth than cold, even far up in my tower chambers. Though my hunger was assuaged, I am still restless and loath to return to my bed and the female reclined on it.

She is fair and delightfully lusty, a quality which I cherish and enjoy above all else in a woman, more even than her name—which for the life of me I cannot remember. Some Countess or another... they all blur together after a while. I remember a touch, a gasp, a blush, the bite of nails in my shoulder, the shocked cry of unexpected pleasure. These are things to savor. Names change. Memories... ah, memories are what I live for.

I trace the gilded title of the book beneath my hand and smile. Yes, memories make such delightful companions.

"Come to bed," the female mewls as though I am a servant to do her bidding.

"No," I say. She is a leech. If I come near enough to touch, she will latch on to any part of me she can reach and cling like second skin. I hoped the binds would dissuade her. Instead, the moment I released her I found myself smothered by quivering arms and ample bosoms. She nearly broke my neck. I am not keen on repeating the experience.

"But I want you to."

"Yes, and were I a better man that would mean something to me. Alas, I am not."

She makes another mewling sound. "But Bastien... don't you love your Christine anymore?"

A stronger puff of air brings with it a hint of pine trees. I inhale deeply of the mysterious scent of silence and turn to the mirror to see my own mocking smirk. "I never claimed to love you at all."

Christine giggles and a scowl replaces my smirk. "Play your games, my love, but we both know that before the night is through, you will be back in my arms, thrusting that glorious, hard cock between my thighs." She slides off the bed and comes to me, snaking her pale arms around my bare waist. Her hands splay over my stomach as she catches my eye in the mirror and smiles. "And we will both adore it."

We make a stunning portrait in the mirror's frame—she, a soft, pliant beauty with hair the color of sable, and I, the golden god.

Christine, I remember now, is a conquest if ever there was one. Daughter of a well-to-do man, betrothed to a well-to-do noble; she used to be a pious, virtuous woman. Now her greedy fingers slip down over the hard ridges of my abdomen to curl around my rising cock. Her generous breasts are pressed into my back and she writhes against me, so eager to seduce though her skill is sadly lacking. No doubt I will find her already wet and aching for me.

I have well and truly corrupted her. I could not be more proud. She sees my smile and returns it. "Shall we?" she asks boldly, but her eyes betray uncertainty.

Well, we can't have that, can we? I drag her hands away before she chokes the life out of my most favorite body part and turn to capture her mouth. She moans eagerly, looping her arms around my neck to hoist herself up.

I have different plans. I ravish her mouth, savoring the way her breath catches. Women always interpret these kisses as proof of a man's hunger for them, body and soul. Christine is no different. It works to my advantage—the easier to get under her skirts. In truth, I only want her to stop pestering me with her nonsense. Her mouth is much better suited for other purposes. She is gasping for breath as I back her out to the balcony. The swell of her backside touches the cold stone balustrade, and she emits a squeak that makes me smile against her lips.

I break our kiss long enough for her to look behind her at the vast, dark night and back at me. Her eyes are wide—with wonder or fear, I cannot tell. Nor do I care. "Turn around," I say.

Christine licks her lips and hesitates, but she does as she's told. I taught her to trust in that which only I can give her. I lean her over the balustrade. It's wide enough to support her, the edge just brushing the underside of her breasts. I nudge her legs apart and press into her, palming her curves for leverage. I take her slowly at first, to give her a moment to appreciate the breathless thrill of vertigo. But soon I am thrusting hard and deep, and she's screaming her pleasure into the dawn as her body squeezes me tight as a fist.

I take her until she is too weak to move; bring her pleasure so intense it doesn't stop even when I have. She comes apart in my arms as I carry her back inside, and again as I dress her in one of my robes. She cannot keep her feet under her on the way down the staircase. Her smile is blissful and utterly oblivious. I place her gently on the plush seat of my carriage, and her nails curl into my arm as another climax shudders through her. She is still coming when I kiss her good-bye, and when her eyes once more open half mast, she looks at me as though I am an angel flown down from the heavens.

I close and latch the black lacquered door painted with my golden crest and tell my driver to deposit her home. He doesn't look me in the eye when he answers, "Yes, my Lord Bastien." He knows better than to protest my wishes. He will drive the lovely Christine to her father's estate and deliver her, still quivering in my robe, directly into his arms.

Chapter Two

A week has gone by and no one has appeared on my doorstep to challenge me. I take it as a sign Christine's family has decided to bear their humiliation in private to preserve the marriage contract. A shame, really. A proper duel would go a long way to relieving this wretched ennui.

It's at times like these I miss the court. There, at least, the air was fragrant with intrigue and politics. I could walk into a room and have every set of eyes turn my way. I had only to smile and a wave of hissing whispers passed through the crowd. It's a mark of a true spy when he can be recognized as one and manage to glean scandalous secrets out of everyone regardless.

Perhaps I should send a missive to Arnaud. Of course, he won't allow me anywhere near his court again without a very public apology, and that I will never do. It's not my fault the courtiers made a confessionary of me for the pleasure of my bed. If they did not want their secrets revealed, they shouldn't have whispered them in my ear.

I sigh with only the slightest of regrets as I stand before a bookcase in my library, a glass of wine in one hand and Madame Bordeaux's book in the other, wondering where to catalog her chronicles. The volume deserves a place of honor, if for no other reason than it being dedicated to me. And the fact that I feature rather prominently between its pages. The lady, of course, had impeccable manners and didn't name any of her lovers. Nevertheless, she did personally deliver an autographed copy of her book to each of us as a memento of our time together.

My dedication reads, *To my Lord Bastien, with fond memories of the nights we spent together and covetous wishes for more.* A fond smile brings something akin to warmth to the barren cockles of my unused heart at the teasing reminder of her graceful *coup de grâce*.

I remember the night I met the lovely Madame. I was drunk on a new shipment of the smoothest Bordeaux I've ever tasted and on the prowl for an able bodied companion to share it with. I stepped rather precariously into the establishment, proclaiming myself to be High King Cocksworth the Ravisher and demanding a virgin to be sacrificed on my majestic blow horn. The scene was later described to me in great detail by several of the helpful lads who attempted to remove me from the building.

"Stop!" a commanding and distinctly female voice cried. I looked up, blinked past the blur of inebriation to behold an angel in a silk gown of such deep red it was nearly black. She glided down the staircase and dismissed my manhandlers with nothing more than a regal nod. "Come with me," she said, and like a lost pup I followed her obediently back to her chamber.

She introduced herself as the Madame and refused to give her real name. I'll freely admit I was not at my sharpest that night, but I found myself intrigued by the lady. Every attempt at learning her true identity was met with craft and wit and for an hour at least we engaged in a bout of verbal fencing I've never experienced before or since. Coy is not a word to describe her. She was masterful, yes. Charming beyond measure, enticing and earthy, but never coy. Men loved her because she loved them, it was as simple as that.

On that night, with a half empty bottle of spirits in my hand and much more of it in my belly, I named her Madame Bordeaux. Her laugh was a delightfully gutsy, artless sound that invited me to join her, unlike the tittering of overbred young maidens.

The Beast Series

I like to think it was a stroke of destiny that hers was the brothel I stumbled into that night. Her tutelage proved to be most... enlightening. Madame Bordeaux took great pride in her work. The art of pleasure was her passion and in that quest, nothing was too sacred, nothing was forbidden. We found in each other a counterpart most willing to dive into anything head first or arse backward and jointly devoted two blissful years to the study of the limits of human pleasure. Then she kindly and with infinite grace broke off our relationship, and we went our separate ways.

If pressed, I would say I miss her.

I set my glass on the floor and pull several tomes from the shelf closest to eye level, tossing them carelessly to the ground. When half of it is clear, I separate the remainder of the books and push them to either edge. Madame Bordeaux's volume takes its rightful place in the center, with the cover facing outward.

I trace the gilded lettering. Selfish bitch. She was the picture of pleasance the day she delivered her gift. She offered smiles and platitudes, politely declining my invitation to tea, supper, or sex. The woman presented me with the book, kissed my cheek and got back into her carriage, waving good-bye as it rolled away.

Two weeks later a nameless child messenger informed me the Madame had succumbed to consumption. She never said a word, not one indication she might be in need of assistance. If nothing else, I could have made her final days the most beautiful of her life. But in all our time together, she never asked for anything. And I never did offer. Ours was a simple relationship, based on our mutual respect for each other's remove. Our shared interest in sex and easy conversation was, in fact, all we ever shared of ourselves.

After five years I still wonder whether the reason she never told me about her illness was because she expected me to turn her away. The thought has me reaching for my glass once more.

"Bastien, you amoral bastard, where the hell are you?"

I need not even raise an eyebrow at that insolent below. As the footsteps rush past the library door, I whistle loudly to announce myself. The intruder returns and the door pushes open. "Ah, there you are. At your books again? Good God, you must be bored out of your mind."

I look over my shoulder at him. "And it's a pleasure to see you, too, old friend."

'm here to rescue you out of this dreary prison. ...nto town tonight." Louis Lafarge, son and heir ...is the closest thing to my equal within miles. His ...granted the lands on the other side of Fauve, which ...illage with grain.

...s and I understand each other on a level not many others can ...sp. Where I have a thought, I find Louis is already putting it into action. Where he has a hankering for a raucous adventure, I know just where to find it. He was the one who explained to me the merits of spying at court—and also the one who got me in trouble for it. But what's a little scandal between friends? The one thing I can always count on with Louis is that he will rather start a peasant rebellion than let either of us wallow in boredom.

A man could not ask for a better comrade.

"Another night of sin and debauchery?" I ask.

He grins and says, "Better. *Mon ami*, this night will change your life!"

"I can hardly wait," I say dryly, but find myself rousing to the prospect of something new. In these isolated parts, any novelty is a thing to be savored. One never knows when another might happen by. I call for my carriage to be prepared while I dress and fill a pouch with coin and a bauble or two. Like novelties, women are to be grasped whenever possible, and nothing snares one's eye better than the glitter of gem and gold. I have a chest full of them for precisely that purpose.

"Another night out, my Lord?" Jacques inquires as I pass him in the great hall. His nose is uncharacteristically in the air. My butler and head of my household is impeccably trained to keep his goddamned mouth shut. Whatever has him in a snit should not matter to me in the least, and yet I discover that my mood is souring, which only serves to anger me.

"Is there something requiring my attention?" I snap.

"A messenger from Lady Christine's father brought this note." He offers it on a silver platter, already opened. "It would seem the engagement is broken. As you may know, the Count puts on great appearances, but is deeply in debt and in dire need of the coin the marriage contract would have brought to his coffers. Now that it is not to be, he inquires as to your intentions toward his daughter. Her reputation is of a great concern to him."

The Beast Series

His coffers are most likely the greater concern. I scowl at the bu[tler,] pointedly avoiding my gaze. Snatching up the letter, I crumple it in[to] a ball and toss it on the hearth fire. "The short answer, Jacques, wa[s] 'no, my Lord Bastien.'"

He bows away without a word.

"Bastien!" Louis calls impatiently.

I snarl at nothing and follow him out to the carriage.

Chapter Three

Our usual haunt is The Howling Monkey. It is an establishment of questionable repute, to be sure, but the tavern is always well stocked and the inn's rooms are decently appointed and usually clean. The owner, a pot-bellied, balding man with half his teeth missing, greets us as soon as we enter. He knows us—we pay well for his silence.

"I see you've invited more company," I tell Louis, seeing a number of familiar faces among the patrons here.

"The more the merrier," Louis assures me. He has, in fact, invited several more of his circle. I find no fault with his choices.

Young Firmin has an ill advised penchant for gambling, not that any of us ever bother to advise. He always knows where the players are rife for fleecing. It is his execution that usually falls short. Even now he has his marked deck of cards laid out on the table, practicing sleight of hand which will get one of his appendages cut off at some point.

Gaspard and Edgard are twin cloth merchants who spend their days ogling half naked women through a peep hole. They are young

enough to be shy around females, and for that I am inclined to
look their deviance. Though I have offered to introduce them
women well versed in handling inexperienced men, they obstinate
insist they can find their own whores.

Adrien is the reasonable one of the lot. Besides me, he can most
easily talk us out of trouble with the more respectable denizens with
whom we share this world. Unbeknownst to said denizens, he is also
the most wicked, with proclivities even I sometimes question.

And then there are the ladies of our company. Liliane, Honorine,
Brigitte, and Adeline. One lovelier than the next. Wicked, wicked
creatures the lot of them. I could paint their bodies with my eyes
closed—and have, on occasion, done just that. Liliane and Brigitte
are femme fatales in the making. The moment their fathers are gone
and buried, I fully expect them to go gallivanting into the world
without a care for consequence. Adeline makes true the saying that
quiet waters run deep. She keeps her own counsel because she stutters when she finds herself the center of attention. What she lacks as
a conversationalist, she makes up for with ardor. A brilliant strategist, in bed and out of it. True to her name, Honorine is a virgin. We
allow her among us because ... well, I'm not quite sure why. She is a
tease of the vilest kind. I suppose that endears her to me quite a bit.

"The Fellowship of Depravity convenes once again," I note.

"Bastien," Liliane greets with a saucy grin and wink.

I bow to them all, and when Adeline offers her hand, I take it, pull
her close and kiss her cheek. "Good evening, my Lord," she says.

"Good evening, my dear," I reply.

The serving wenches load our table with ale, obliging us to stay a
while. It would be rude to refuse, and so we amuse ourselves until
nightfall with drink and a friendly game of cards. We do not play for
money but for favors. Rarely does anyone collect on them. If we did,
Firmin would be my slave for the rest of his life, and I would have to
clean out Louis' stables for a year.

The men may know their tricks, but it would take a stronger man
than any of us to keep his focus against the wiles of our womenfolk.

My hand is good, and with a little playacting I can convince the
others that it is even better. I am preparing to do so when Honorine
says, "I want to raise the wager." Just the way she says this has all of
us rapt on her. She smiles and traces the neckline of her low cut
gown. "I wish to wager my virginity."

dies fold, whispering their jokes behind raised looks at us men. Six of us against Honorine she doesn't intend to win. Adrien winces and ds cards on the table face down. "Gentlemen, good

narrows her eyes at him but doesn't comment.

n loses the next hand and is disqualified. Louis and Edgard at out Gaspard and my hand takes out Louis. Honorine is still in the game. The next hand I am dealt is shite. Which is not to say I cannot win, only that it will take considerable effort. Edgard is sweating and Honorine is looking at me the way I've seen her covet a pastry she cannot have.

If I bluff, I can eliminate Edgard and play Honorine alone. The question is whether the prize would be worth the effort. And, should the unlikely happen and I lose, what will she demand as her due? The thought of putting the little trouble maker in her place is tempting enough that, for a moment, I contemplate making a real play for her. It only lasts for that moment. As enjoyable as it would be to knock Mademoiselle Saintly off her pedestal, I can already see resentment on the faces of the others. She will never acquiesce to anything less than an honest tryst and no sooner than on her wedding day. This is all a ploy to get us riled and sic us against each other.

A woman was never worth the price of friendship.

I play perhaps the first honest game of my life. No tricks, no cheats. I play the hand I was given, knowing I will lose. Edgard's hand takes the game and I am out. I feign disappointment and remove myself to the bar for a stronger drink while they finish the final round.

Adeline follows me. "He is a fool," she says. "I am glad you let him win."

"You presume me immune to Honorine's charms?"

"I know you to be." Her fingers travel over my arm. "Innocence was never a lure for you, not even m-mine."

Adeline was an innocent the first time she rode alone through the night, slipped into my castle and beneath my bed sheets. Innocent in body, perhaps, but in no other way. I was the one seduced. The reminder makes me chuckle. I take her fingers in my hand. "I've always wondered just how innocent you really were," I say. "And what precisely did you tell Honorine about that night to mak[e] stoop to this?"

Surprise, guilt, and finally hurt flash in her lovely eyes. She mas[ks] them quickly with an easy smile. "A right p-p-proper bastard yo[u] are. It is your good fortune that you are this handsome; otherwise, no one would be able to t-tolerate you at all."

I salute her with my glass. "But you did not contradict me."

A cheer goes up when Edgard wins. We both turn to watch everyone congratulate him while Honorine sits quietly possessed with her hands in her lap. Not surprisingly, the moment the rowdy group quiets, Honorine demurs and begs release from her wager.

Bastards we may be, but beasts we are not. Faced with a lady's—and I use the term lightly—distress, Edgard relents.

Honorine smiles with relief and gratitude. She has no notion of what enemies she just made of all of us.

Adrien clears his throat. "It is time," he says. "Shall we say our prayers now or later?"

Louis waves him on, and the rest of us bow our heads.

"Dear God, we humbly ask that you grant us wisdom to find trouble where it hides, strength to venture forth into it, turn of phrase to ease those disturbed sensitivities which can be eased, and coin to pay off those which cannot. Forgive us for the sins which we are about to commit and for not including you in them."

My mouth twitches with suppressed laughter. I solemnly intone, "Your prayers are heard. Go forth and sin, my children."

"Amen!"

"Where shall we do our sinning?" Brigitte asks eagerly.

"That, my dear, is a surprise," Louis answers. "You wouldn't believe me if I told you. No, this is something you all must see for yourselves."

Adeline shivers and loops her arm through mine. "I do love a good mystery," she says.

"Fellows, let us take the night by the horns!"

Chapter Four

Louis leads the way through town. The village of Fauve is far removed from this place, yet I could easily call it home. Cobblestoned streets weave between buildings tall enough to have three rows of windows. No thatched roofs here, all are covered with sturdy shingles.

We walk at a brisk pace. There are still merchants about, finishing their final tasks of the day and closing their shops for the night. They are not welcoming of our presence, but as long as we don't disturb them, the townsfolk are willing to tolerate us for the coin we always leave in our wake.

Louis leads us all the way to the edge of town, where the cobblestones level out into stomped dirt and the houses become smaller and older. Not far off is a Gypsy village. I can hear the drums and fiddles from here. This is as near civilization as the Gypsies are willing to come. Many still wander in the way of their people, but most have settled here, in wagons turned into shacks, built up into what might pass for an abode. Fires are lit in the distance, perhaps some sort of celebration. Of what, I don't know. Then again, Gypsies don't usually need a reason.

We stop before a shack consisting of four separate walls h[...]
gether by rope and covered with oiled cloth. In front of the c[...]
which serves as a door sits a hunched woman in a cloak. An old [...]
rel stands as her table, and on top of it is a deck of cards. Her ho[...]
is so large it covers her face. I see nothing of her except her hands,
one smooth and young, the other gnarled and old.

"What is this, Louis?" I ask, unnerved by the sight of an old woman. "Have you suddenly developed a taste for the arcane?"

He laughs. "This is merely the…"

A single gnarled finger rises to point at my chest, and the air is suddenly too thick to breathe. The woman gathers her cards and places them face down on one edge of the barrel. They somehow hover nearly half over that edge without tipping over.

Adeline clutches my arm. "Bastien?" she says uncertainly. I can't find my voice to reassure her.

"Is this part of the game?" Adrien asks.

"No," Louis says. "Last time wasn't… she didn't…"

The hag slams her old hand on top of the barrel, demanding silence. With her young hand, she takes cards off the top of the deck and arranges them in a circle.

"Listen, we just want to enter," Louis says.

The hag holds up a young finger in a staying gesture and indicates the spread with her old.

"What is she doing?" Adeline asks, half hiding behind me. Under normal circumstances I would laugh at her and extricate myself from her hold. At the moment, I am too unsettled to speak a single word. The hag pointed at me, she is looking at me. Whatever fortune she is about to divine is mine. I don't want to see it. With everything in me I dread the first card being flipped. But for the life of me I cannot look away.

The smooth hand of youth reaches gracefully for the card farthest from her and flips it. The card says *Wheel of Fortune* and at its center is a golden wheel of the Zodiac, with star constellations clearly marked around it. It's upside down.

"It would seem the odds are not in your favor," Louis says. He sounds bored.

I dare not breathe as the withered hand reaches for the second card in the circle. Judgment. Also reversed. A set of scales tipped on

...m the makeshift table and as I am staring at it, ...rd breaks before my eyes. This is a hallucina-... drunk, or perhaps it's a trick of light and the ...hole.

...s in my throat and I cannot clear it. I choke on the ...nhale as the third card is turned. The Hermit. Nothing ... a hooded figure, hunched the same way as this hag who ...es to know my destiny. And the scales of Justice tip the other ..ay.

I can't blink, or turn away. My companions are gone. I am alone in the night, the darkness drowning me in this magic. There is nothing but me, and the cards, and the hands turning them. My gaze is rapt on the next card to be turned over. The Moon. All the faces suddenly shift, moving now with a life of their own and, while the moon changes phases, the hunched figure of the hermit grows and tears at its cloak, revealing a monster underneath.

My heart races, aching in my chest, and I can hear my own breath wheeze in and out of me on a feral growl. The hag pauses with her smooth hand hovering over the fifth card. She waits as though for divine guidance, her hooded head cocking slightly to the side. She dips a slow nod and flips the card—Strength. A crimson rose blooms on it, its thorns long and needle sharp. The hag's hand passes over the card a second time and the rose is gone. In its place stands a woman, naked as the day she was born, yet standing tall and straight, looking right at me with a challenge in her eyes. *I will not yield*, her eyes say, and it makes me feel weak. *She* makes me feel weak.

A whirlwind rises around me, so powerful I'm afraid it will lift me off my feet, and I don't understand how the cards can be so still on that barrel, so steady, as if my future is already written in stone and it's only my denial that tries to make me stray from the path set out before me. I fight it with all of my might. There is wilderness ahead, danger I can avoid if only I turn my feet around and go back the way I came.

The pull of destiny and my need to escape it tears me asunder, and in my mind I scream for the hag to turn the last card. Finish this—save me somehow.

She does, and everything stills once more. Breath leaves me, as desperate to escape as my own soul. The card is Death. The salvation I demanded stares at me from black holes in a bare skull. This card doesn't move; doesn't change. It is absolute.

The previous fervor of my heartbeat stops completely and I clutch my chest, the barrel, anything to regain some semblance of steadiness. As my heart lurches back to life, I tear my gaze away from my own demise and just catch a glint of obsidian in the hag's eye through a hole in her hood. I find no sympathy there.

"Right," Louis says. "This has been entertaining, but we've tarried long enough." The hag turns to him as he reaches into his jacket pocket and pulls out a card of his own. Holding it up for the hag to see, he places it into the center of the barrel. Ten of Pentacles.

The hag straightens and becomes all business, pointing to each of us in turn before tapping the card on which ten silver coins glint merrily. The toll must be paid before we are allowed to pass. Each of us pays the coin she demands and only after she's pocketed her due does she rise from her seat and pull aside the curtain door.

Louis grins. "After you," he invites.

The women pair off with the men and enter arm in arm through the door. Adeline, who released me and took shelter in Adrien's arms when the Death card was flipped, looks back at me before she disappears through the door. Only Louis and I are left. I hesitate before stepping through the veil. I try to catch the hag's eye, but can no longer find it in the shadows of her hood. She is a statue, as still and uninterested as stone.

Having no other choice I step into the darkness of the shack...

... and emerge on the other side into blinding light. For a moment I can see nothing but bright colors swirling around me. I hear voices as delicate as bell chimes and music as sweet as honey mead. I am not in the Gypsy village anymore, nor any other place in existence. Before me is a dream, a fantasy given shape.

Behind me, Louis claps me on the shoulder. "My lords and ladies of the Fellowship of Depravity," he says, "Welcome to the Faery court."

Chapter Five

The cards are instantly forgotten. The door through which we entered is gone, vanished into thin air and all around me is pandemonium, a cornucopia of creatures from myth and legend. Three girls dance around the gathering, holding hands. It is only when I look closer that I realize how my eyes have deceived me. They aren't holding hands—they have no hands at all. Rather, their arms are joined together at the wrist so as to make one creature of three.

Not far away, a stunningly beautiful woman covered only with vines and leaves cuddles three ghostlike lizards. They notice my regard and unfurl massive wings, baring rows of sharp teeth in warning. The woman hisses and disappears.

I spin in baffled circles as my mind struggles to make sense of this. Over there, a tall, handsome pair. Their skin is gray, their hair white as snow, and everywhere their bare feet touch, frost blooms across the ground. On the other side, a woman with hair literally made of gold. Behind her, a behemoth of a man; a monster with horns flowing from his temples, back along his head. His legs are like that of an animal, and giant bat wings are folded against his bare back. Right before me, a red haired woman laughs and twirls, faster and faster until she bursts into flames and burns away. As her ashes rain down, they swirl closer and tighter, growing thick with smoke until it solidifies and pales, and the woman is back again, dancing off somewhere else.

My companions have left me. They are scattered everywhere, as awestruck as I, approaching creatures with caution. Only Louis remains, a smug smirk on his face. "Well?"

"What is this? Where have you brought us?"

Louis grabs my shoulders and gives me a shake. "To Eden, my boy. Now stop gaping like an imbecile and enjoy! I want to introduce you to our hostess. She is... perfect." He sounds like a green lad talking about a sweetheart.

I look for Adrien to reason me out of this madness. He is reclined on a bed of moss with a pale haired temptress feeding him grapes. Adeline is in the arms of the bat winged monster, dancing. The twins are watching the gray couple create ice sculptures out of thin air. I've lost sight of the others.

Somehow a flower shaped cup appears in my hand. "Go on," Louis says. "Have a sip. I guarantee you've never tasted anything like it." He toasts me with a drink of his own.

The chalice in my hands is alive, a real flower with petals soft as silk and glowing amber liquid inside. I am mesmerized by the sight of it. I take a sip, taste the sweet, thick nectar and sway on my feet. Head spinning, I look around again with dream hazed eyes. Suddenly everything makes sense as though I've known this place all my life. I am in the Faery court. I laugh. "Well done, Louis!"

A figure slams into me, turning me sideways. The woman spins around so fast she becomes invisible, and before I know up from down again, my back is against the wall and a shining silver blade is pressed against my throat. The attacker has hair as black as a crow's feather and eyes red as fire. She is dressed in what looks like black ribbons wound around her body. She is furious, much stronger than she appears, and I have nothing to defend myself with. Even if I did, I suspect it would do no good against this creature so I hold still and try to appear harmless. The female bares her teeth at me and releases me with a huff. The ends of her ribbons trail after her as she walks away. She leaves bloody footprints behind.

"I see you've met Discord."

Louis straightens and his eyes grow wide. He smiles like a child presented with a new toy and bows deeply to the newcomer. "My Lady."

The woman is perhaps the only creature dressed as a human. Her gown is a simple sheath of silk, her hair is half braided around her head and flows down her back. She is beyond beautiful. When she smiles I feel as though the sun has risen and I am blinded. No wonder Louis is so smitten with her.

Louis shoves at me. I remember myself and take a bow. "My Lady," Louis says, "allow me to introduce my best friend, Lord Bastien Sauvage."

"I am Lilith. And Louis didn't tell me he was bringing such lively company with him." The reprimand is delivered so gracefully I almost miss it.

Louis seems dumbfounded and a little pale. If I know my friend, and I do, it never even occurred to him that we might not be welcome here. "You must forgive him," I say. "He was utterly smitten at first sight of you and since then completely forgot himself. Now, having seen you for myself, I understand just how he feels."

Lilith is lithe in form, nearly of a height with me. Her hair is the color of sun and her eyes shine pale like stars. Inhuman. Inhumanly beautiful. God could not have created this creature; she is too perfect a temptation. I find I am not interested in resisting her.

Louis clears his throat. "Right you are, Bastien."

Lilith ignores him. "Charming," she says to me. "Bastien, was it? Well, Bastien, you may come with me. This is a tea party compared to what I have planned for tonight. Perhaps we can see if you live up to your name, Savage."

She offers her hand and I take it.

"But my Lady... Lilith!"

"You can entertain yourself for a while, can't you, Louis?" she says without even bothering to look his way. "Corral that pack of animals you brought with you. This one I wish to keep an eye on myself."

I put on my most charming smile. "I am at your service, Lilith."

"Indeed you are." Her tone makes me smile. I know what to expect from this one. And I cannot wait.

She leads me through a curtain of willow branches and the world changes again. Here, the lights are dim and everything is in shades of red and black. Fires burn in pits and around them piles of pillows are strewn about. There are creatures here, too. Most of them are writhing together in a tangle of limbs and appendages to a chorus of sighs and moans. The aura of sex and otherworldly magic brushes against my skin, inside my clothes, and makes me unsteady on my feet.

I drink deeply of the nectar I still have and with each swallow I feel more at ease. When my cup is empty, another replaces it. Hands reach out to me and pull back again. Covetous gazes follow me as Lilith leads the way through the throng to a bower in the center. The pillars are reedy trees and the roof is made of spider webs.

Once past the circle of pillars, the empty spaces between them fill with a reflective watery film. I am encased in a mirror box and all around me my doubles stare seemingly everywhere at once. I turn to the closest one. It doesn't turn with me. I touch the surface, tracing my profile as my rippling reflection reaches out to something else.

Lilith appears next to me. Her dress is gone and she is naked, her loose hair creating a curtain to hide her nudity. She touches my shoulder and my clothing, too, disappears. She hands me another cup, this one black. "Beautiful, is it not?" She tunnels a hand beneath the fall of her hair and moves it over her shoulder, baring her rounded breast. "We are completely alone. No one will dare disturb us here." She raises the cup in my hand to my mouth and tips it.

I drink and nearly choke on the first swallow. This is no nectar. It tastes sharp as lightning caught in a cup. My insides turn hot with it. Lilith takes the delicate chalice from me and tugs me to the pillows. I am on my back and my head is spinning, but my cock is hard and straining toward the welcoming heat of Lilith where she hovers so close above me. She kisses me, her hand strokes me and I groan into her mouth.

Lust is too tame a word for what I feel. I am on fire, desperate for release, suffocating. Air does not exist unless I'm kissing her. She laughs when I fist my hands in her hair and roll until she is pinned beneath me. Her laugh turns into a moan when I thrust into her to the hilt. My back bows with the pleasure of it and I turn into a rutting animal, the savage she named me.

Her limbs loop around me and she arches closer as I piston in and out of her. Her skin is like the silk she wore to hide it, cool to the touch but searing like a brand. Her nails are claws that leave bloody scratches in my back, but with a caress of her palm she takes the sting away. In the mirrors I can see the skin heal without a mark left behind. I see us together, my own arse and back, her legs shifting restlessly, hungry for more, just as I am.

My muscles strain and I give her all I have, and when her climax lifts both of us into the air, she drags me right after her into the most intense ecstasy I have ever felt. I am weightless, formless. I am nothing but euphoria and starlight. When I return to myself, I ache everywhere.

Another black cup presses to my lips. "Drink, lover," Lilith purrs. "We are nowhere near finished." As the liquid pours down my raw throat, her mouth travels over me. She tastes herself on my cock, still hard and ready, takes it into her mouth deep ... so deep. I roar while she sucks me into another climax and am more than happy to return the favor before I mount her again. And again. And again.

Time means nothing. Another black cup, another whisper of praise, a demand for more, harder, *now*. I am helpless not to give. She robs me of everything and when I am exhausted, too weak to continue, presses another cup to my lips. It is an elixir of everlasting fuck. I don't care where it keeps coming from or even what it is. All that matters is that while I am drinking it I can keep going as long as I want. And I want more.

Lilith laughs and lets me indulge, luxuriate in her body or fuck it any way I want. Her pleasure becomes mine and everything I am is hers. "More," I snarl against her neck. "More, more..." the words punctuate each of my thrusts. Her limbs quiver as she clutches me. So do mine. She doesn't scream her pleasure, she sighs it, and with that one breath steals my soul.

I fall back onto the pillows, gasping for air, reaching for that black cup which is sure to appear. Instead I see Lilith's face hovering over me. Her eyes shine brighter than ever, her lips red as blood—red *with* blood. "Humans break so easily," she murmurs with regret and leans down to press a soft kiss to my lips. I reach for her to deepen it, but she holds me back. Instead of a black cup, a white one appears in her hand and she eases an arm beneath my shoulders to help me drink from it.

An unbearable heaviness permeates me from head to toe. With her soft whispers in my ear telling me to rest now, I let my eyes close and embrace the waiting darkness.

Chapter Six

I dream the world as a painted tarot card. The moon bulges full in the night sky, and all the stars are traced into constellations. A wolf sits on the cliff before me, howling soundlessly. Roses and dark cloaks swirl around me, a black cup spills shimmering liquid into the grass, and then a woman appears before me. She is slight, naked, and so close to me we are nearly toe to toe. Her hair is a lush reddish brown, a shade so warm and inviting I want to sift my fingers through it.

She is a painting that is somehow not a part of this world. I recognize her for the innocent she is by her wide blue eyes, at once challenging and pleading with me. Something inside my chest clenches tight. I want to touch her, draw her into my arms. I am certain the smallest contact will melt away the paint and make her as real as I am. She is made to fit me and I can almost feel her skin against mine as I reach out.

But I pull back. What if I'm wrong? That single touch could destroy her. She stands before me, an angel, warm and good in a way I have never been. She might as well be the world away. It maddens me. Her mouth moves and I strain to hear her words, but there is nothing. "What?" I demand. "What do you want!"

My bellow frightens her and she is gone.

"No, wait! Come back!"

Blood red rose petals rain down where she stood. I stoop to pick one up and it withers in the palm of my hand. "Come back," I plead.

I wake on a bed of white pillows, fully dressed. I am in Lilith's bower, but she is gone. There are no more mirrors, the fires have gone out, and the creatures around them lie motionless, asleep. My head is splitting. I try to retrace my steps back to my friends, but as soon as I leave the circle of trees I find myself in front of the shack.

The hag stands by the door which is once again covered with the curtain. "Where are my friends?" My voice is raw, hardly recognizable.

The hag says nothing.

"Are they still inside?"

She proffers her hand. In the palm of it is the damned tarot deck.

"Why will you not speak, damn you?"

The hag flips the top card. The Hierophant. Whatever the hell that means. I shake my head and grasp the curtain to go back inside. Louis and the others can probably take care of themselves much better than I can at the moment, but I still need to find them.

An old, gnarled hand curls painfully in my forearm, stopping me in my tracks. When I turn back to her, the hag brushes the top card off the deck and flips the next one. "The Devil?" I stare at her for an explanation.

She simply drops that card and flips the next one. Strength. "Yes, you said that last night," I say dryly. "Show me something new."

The cards shoot off her hand, straight at me. I fall back with a shout, flailing and slapping them away without success. They batter my face like so many bird wings and, for a moment, I am deaf and blind to the world at large. When the assault stops, I shove to my feet, ready to strangle the bitch.

She is gone.

I circle the shack to look for her and find nothing. I tear the curtain off the door, but there is nothing inside other than stomped dirt and four rickety walls. No more Faery court, and no friends. In my hasty backward retreat I bump into the barrel. I reach for it to steady myself and feel a prick in my palm.

A blood red rose lies on the makeshift table, placed next to a neat stack of tarot cards.

There is no one around to see me pocket the cards. I hesitate before I pick up the rose and inhale its fragrance. It's just like the one on the Strength card. *Strength.* I scoff at that and toss the bloom aside. Shoving my hands into my pockets, I head back into town to my waiting carriage.

Only my carriage is not waiting, and when I inquire as to its whereabouts, the merchants prove less than obliging. My pockets empty of coin, I am forced to walk home. It was an hour's ride in a carriage, it takes me half the day to get back to my castle, and by then I am ready to throttle my driver and skin him while his legs still twitch.

When I open my own front door, I find my companions from last night have my butler cornered by the hearth. They seem very angry, but I can't tell what they're all shouting about at the same time.

What the hell do they want now? My ear splitting whistle breaks up the lynch mob and the entry hall falls silent. Everyone is staring at me.

"Bastien!" Adeline cries and launches herself at me. Honorine and Brigitte are weeping. Liliane is not even there.

"Holy Christ, man," Adrien says, raking his hair back. "We thought you were dead."

I stare at him and then look down at Adeline making a mess of my shirt. "What? Adeline, let go of me. If this is a joke it's not funny. You bastards not only left me there, you took my goddamned carriage! Would it have killed you to wait until morning?"

Adrien and Louis exchange a look as Adeline rejoins them, her face flushed with tears and a healthy dose of embarrassment. Good. "Bastien," Adrien says, "you've been gone for two weeks."

Jacques bows impassively and removes himself from my vicinity. Clever man. Louis looks torn between confusion and anger. Edgard and Firmin are staring as if they are seeing a ghost, Adrien and Gaspard both have their arms full of distraught female. They believe what Adrien said.

"Have you all gone insane?"

"Look," Edgard says, pointing at the door. Or rather the window above it.

I look. "What, the moon?"

"It was new when we went to the Faery court."

It's full now. My throat closes shut and I have to swallow repeatedly to find my voice again. "Where is Liliane?" I don't dare look at them for the answer.

"She's gone, Bastien," Firmin says. "She took up with a... creature. She was dead when we found her."

I shudder. Two weeks. Liliane is dead. My chest feels hollow. I rub at it and find the stolen tarot deck. If I take it out right now and look at the top card, will it be Death again? Was the hag trying to warn me?

"Leave," I say.

Firmin escorts Honorine and Brigitte to the carriage. Edgard and Gaspard follow, with Adrien and Adeline taking up the rear. Adeline touches my arm and looks at me sadly as she passes by. I wince and pull away.

Only Louis remains. After the others are gone down the long drive, he says, "It must have been an accident. They don't... they don't murder out of spite. The male probably didn't realize how fragile she was. You know Liliane, she'd go toe to toe with the Devil to prove that she could."

He says it too easily, as if he is inured to this sort of thing happening. How often has he been there? How well does he truly know those creatures? How many has he seen die at their hands?

"What did she say to you?" he asks. "Lilith."

"There really wasn't much talking, Louis," I reply.

Louis takes an angry step, as though to challenge me. It takes me by surprise. Of all of us, I would never expect Louis to be the one who takes exception to what I do, or with whom. "She was mine," he grates. "You selfish, narcissistic prig, she was mine!"

"Apparently, you failed to make her aware of that."

Louis' fist connects with my jaw, spinning me sideways. Half my face goes numb and in an instant explodes in pain. I am so startled I laugh, and once I've started I cannot stop. Seeing Louis' livid face only makes me laugh harder.

He slams the door behind him.

My laughter refuses to subside. My sides hurt from it as I lean against the wall and slide down to the floor, lost in my mirth. Maids poke their heads around corners, servants stare as they pass me by.

It is Jacques who finally scrapes up enough courage to come to my aid. He drags me to my feet and guides me up the stairs to my chambers.

It's not until I am shrugging out of my coat that I notice my reflection in the mirror.

There are tears streaked down my face.

Chapter Seven

I spend the following days in morose drunkenness. I invite no company, nor do I accept any. Summer is turning to autumn and the gardeners are out in droves, tending to the flowers. I watch them from my window, absently shuffling the stolen tarot cards.

Every once in a while a card falls out of the deck. More often than not, it's the Strength card, with its red, red rose and sharp thorns. I find myself searching for the woman I glimpsed beneath the rose. She disappeared like a mirage, not just from the card but from my dreams as well. Now I can't even recall her face. I turn the card this way and that, into the light, into shadow, I bend it just short of creasing. Nothing I do changes the image on its face.

Jacques comes in with a food tray. "The cook must be worried about you, he made your favorite."

"The cook made my favorite, the maids change the bedding every day, the hostler comes in every morning to ask if he should prepare a horse for me. What do you think they're all worried about? That I am dying, or that I am not?"

"You are a spirited man who hasn't left his room for six days, my Lord. It is very uncharacteristic of you."

I look away from the garden just so he can see me raise an eyebrow. "One of my friends died… in a horrible accident three weeks ago. Is a man not allowed time to grieve?"

Jacques picks an invisible speck off his sleeve. "As I said, my Lord, it is very uncharacteristic of you."

My teeth grind together at the implications of that answer. "I am beginning to realize my staff is not very fond of their Lord and master," I muse aloud. I never even considered this to be a possibility before. "Do you by chance harbor some wisdom as to why?"

Jacques says nothing.

"I own them. They live in a castle and they're paid well for their service. They're not beaten or abused in any way. What could they possibly have to complain about?"

My butler offers no explanation.

I shrug philosophically. I really do not care enough to press. "I want roses in the garden," I say instead.

"Yes, my Lord. Do you have a particular spot in mind?"

"Yes. Everywhere."

Jacques nods. "I shall inform the head gardener."

Long after he leaves and my tray has gone cold, I am still sitting at that window, counting stars. I don't want to go to sleep. It's become a chore to dream. Either I'm swamped with memories of Lilith and wake up trying to fuck my pillow, or I am lost in the painted tarot world, chasing after a faceless woman dressed in rose petals. Neither is a welcome sight tonight. Lilith never stays long enough to bring me to come, and the strange woman always slips through my fingers and I can never find her.

And then there is the hag. I saw her a few times as well. Half young maiden, half old crone, like a Faery spell gone awry. Her young eye is black as coal. Her old is white, obviously blind. She stares at me, waiting for something. What does she want? My soul? A woman as well versed in the dark arts as she should already know I don't have one.

By midnight I am sure God created woman in order to punish man. I take a candle and go down to the library. There are hundreds of books in here, surely one of them will be able to entertain me until morning. Maybe if I just sleep by the light of day my dreams will be more pleasant. Or at the very least, less exhausting.

I peruse the subjects. History. I will be asleep after two pages. Politics. Only if I want the women in my dreams to band together against me. I pause at Poetry. There are only a couple of volumes in this category, as sentiment is not something I subscribe to. However, desperate times call for insipidity and, given that my only other option is Myth and Folk Tales, I take a book of poetry from the shelves and take a seat on the settee.

The first verse has me rolling my eyes and snapping the book shut.

Drivel. Another man brought to the brink of madness by woman, whining and pining after his tormentor. It's not the sun kissed wheat of the woman's hair, or the cherry red of her lips, or the peach pink of her cheek that bothers me—obviously the man was hungry when he wrote this. It's not even that he describes this after he sneaked into the woman's chamber in the twilight hours to watch her sleep—I can understand that not every man has the ballocks to wake the woman up for what he really wants from her. No, it's the overblown desperation with which he states that without these features he shall cast himself into the sea and shatter his bleeding heart upon the jagged rocks of the shallows.

I don't relish the idea of destroying a book but in this case I make an exception and burn the damned thing in the hearth. Happy to be rid of it, I retrieve the second book of poetry. This one I open with more caution. I am pleasantly surprised to find the poet whining about war instead of a woman, and for the rest of the night I enjoy vivid imagery of severed limbs and spilling guts.

When morning comes, I dress and order my horse prepared. It's time to look in on my companions and find out what happened that night.

Edgard and Gaspard are closest. I find them in their clothier's shop, strangely subdued and reluctant to talk to me. All they say is that they were separated from the group early on and don't remember much of what happened. They are horrible liars and they know it, but no matter what I say, they will not tell me more.

Honorine has left for her uncle's estate a good two weeks' ride south, by the sea. That is what her head of household tells me when I come calling.

Brigitte is nervous during my visit. Her hands shake as she drinks her tea. She doesn't try to seduce me even once. That, more than anything, tells me that something is wrong.

I find Adeline at Adrien's house. As the only child of a senile father, she has more freedom than other young women to do as she pleases. I am not one to judge, nor do I care whose bed the woman chooses to warm. What I find curious is that Adrien tells me straight away he has asked for Adeline's hand and she consented. They are to be married in the spring. After that announcement I don't have the stomach to ask them about the Faery court.

Firmin is in debtors' prison. I am not allowed near him unless it is with a promissory note to pay off his debts. I leave him to his troubles. I have my own to straighten out.

Finally, there is only Louis left. I think long and hard about riding through Fauve to see him. That a man would go to such lengths over a woman as to shun his friend for having slept with her baffles me. I don't even know what Louis is so upset about—we shared women before. Nevertheless, he is upset enough that I know there's little chance he will tell me anything of what's happened that night. No, I will not be going to Louis.

Which means I only have one option left. As the sun begins to set, I ride headlong to the wooden shack and the hag with her tarot deck.

Chapter Eight

The hag is expecting me. A stool is set before the barrel and she has her cards in hand. It looks exactly like the deck I have in my pocket. I take it out, frowning. The curtain door to the Faery court billows with a life of its own, drawing my eye. The cloth is darker than I remember it, more tattered, yet it still won't show even a glimpse of what's behind it. A soft, warm breeze wafts my way, and I could swear it sigh my name.

The hag waves me to sit and flips the top card of her deck. The King of Pentacles.

I shuffle my deck and place it on the barrel. My first card is The Hierophant. I half grin at this odd way of greeting. "I want to know what happened to my friends," I say, already knowing she won't tell me.

She turns the next card and it is The World. A vague answer that still somehow makes sense. The world, the Faery court, did something to them. It certainly changed me, just as Louis said it would.

The curtain snaps and billows in a nonexistent wind, demanding my attention. The tarot deck will not tell me which of the Faery killed Liliane, or why Honorine suddenly felt the need to escape to the sea. To find that out I'll need to ask someone who speaks. "Yes," I say, finding the prospect of stepping foot in that strange land again is not as unwelcome as I expected. "I want to enter the Faery court again."

The hag shakes her head. It's not a refusal, more disbelief. She thinks I'm lying? "I want to know what happened," I repeat.

The hag shakes her head again and points to my cards. I turn the next one. The Queen of Cups. Now the hag nods. The curtain settles, as if satisfied I've made a liar of myself. Even when I try to be noble my true motives betray me. I haven't come all this way to have a tarot conversation with the hag about my companions—who cares? If Louis, my oldest and closest friend is so quick to shun me over a female, then what good are the rest of them?

The hag turns her card. The Fool.

Without a word, I turn mine. The Wheel of Fortune. I suppose I'll have to take my chances, whatever they may be.

The hag turns The Hermit and swivels it around to face me as if to say, "Remember this?"

I do. The monster hiding under a cloak. My card counters it—Strength. There is the rose and the phantom woman who haunts my dreams. I falter as I place the card on the barrel. The hag, too, seems momentarily distracted. She touches the card, tracing its edges with something akin to reverence. This is what I really came here for.

She turns the next card slower. Death.

A chill runs through me and pain blooms in my chest, as though I've been shot. Another warning. I should heed it this time, pick up my deck and go back home. Instead my hand reaches for the next card.

The hag slams her hand down on top of mine. She half bows her head in what might be ascent or defeat and pushes my turned cards back toward me, spreading her deck across the barrel, face down. She picks one of the lot and turns it without pause. The Two of Pentacles.

I grin when she holds out her hand for the payment. Her fee has doubled since the first time. I pay her and collect my cards. As I am rising from my seat and she is pulling back the curtain to allow me entrance, some morbid curiosity compels me to look at the card she didn't want me to see. I turn it on top of the deck. The Lovers.

The hag hisses, the first sound I have heard her make. She knocks the deck from my hands before I can get a good look at the card and pulls the curtain wider open. Enter or go. But leave the deck.

There is nothing waiting for me in my castle except stone walls and bad dreams. I enter.

The Faery court is not as I remember it. There are trees around me now, with bark of unbroken white and leaves so bright green it hurts to look at them. There is no sun in the sky. Rather, it is the sky itself which shines down to illuminate everything. The creatures I saw before are gone. I am alone in the clearing. "Hello?" I call. Only my echo answers me.

"Is anybody there?"

Nothing.

"Lilith!" I try.

A breeze makes the trees sway and their leaves knock together like delicate wind chimes. "Lover," the air whispers around me.

Lilith appears in a flash of light, draped in a gown made of mist. She smiles knowingly and opens her arms to me. "Welcome back."

I swoop her up and kiss her hard, the familiar taste of her tongue in my mouth bringing back memories of euphoric pain. "How could I resist?"

She laughs. "Did you miss me, Bastien?" She asks this as though already anticipating the answer to be yes.

The truth would not please her, and I am not fool enough to voice it. Instead of answering, I grab her leg and loop it around my waist so she can feel me hard against her. "Where is that damned cup?"

Lilith laughs again. She closes my eyes with a kiss on each lid, and when I open them we are in her bower with its false mirrors. A black cup is waiting for me on a pedestal. I set her away and pick it up.

But I hesitate. I look at my own reflection. It's matching me this time. There is the other me, a cup in his left hand when mine is in my right, that selfsame look of stubborn determination is there in his eyes. That same muscle twitches in his jaw. Our clothes melt away as Lilith comes up behind me and presses her mouth to the center of my spine.

My eyelids droop. My reflection's do not. He shakes his head as though in warning, but Lilith already has her hands on my cock and I can't think. I don't want to think. I want to forget everything, lose myself in pleasure for as long as I can, and then sleep. The most vivid dream I had of the beauty from the card was in this bower after Lilith fucked me nearly to death. I need to see her again. Just once.

I drain the black cup with one swallow and give myself over to its burn.

It's worse than before. I know exactly what the elixir is doing to me; feel every little sting, every stutter of my feeble human heart. But the pleasure is greater as well. It's almost beyond bearing, an agony tearing through my body in bone breaking spasms. One cup, two, three... I lose count. I spent two weeks here last time. This time I know it will be longer.

But I will not die. Not before I see her.

When I collapse, broken and bleeding, still craving the hell bitch who has me in her thrall though I can no longer move to claim her, she takes pity on me and gives me the white cup to drink from. She makes me drink it on my own, and I leave bloody fingerprints on the white petals, spilling more out than into my mouth.

I close my eyes, eagerly awaiting my dreams.

But she does not appear. The now familiar painted world welcomes me, the lone wolf howling at the moon, the swirling cloak circling me and the rose blooming before me. The woman isn't there. I pluck the rose from the ground, the thorns gouging holes in my hand. In its place a thorn bush sprouts at my feet, growing and growing until it's taller than I am, the spikes as long as daggers.

I awake alone in the clearing. The sky is dark and the white trees glow like lanterns. There is the doorway and the curtain which shields this hellish place from the rest of the world, and I stumble out through it, seeking the hag.

She is not there.

On the barrel are my tarot cards and another blood red rose.

Chapter Nine

A grain merchant tells me I was in Faery for seventeen days.

A torrential rain accompanies me on the way home, and by the time I get there I am chilled to the bone. I spend the next two weeks battling a fever that has me chasing ghosts all around the castle. Jacques has to restrain me in the night to keep me from wandering out on the balcony after a hallucination.

When the fever breaks I curse the visions which will not return. She was here. I saw her running through the hallways of this castle and, though I never caught her, knowing I had her in my home brought me a sense of tranquility that stilled the fervor of Lilith's influence.

Now she is gone again.

This little obsession is driving me to distraction, and I don't even know why. There was nothing special about the woman I saw in my dreams. She could have been one among thousands, noble or peasant. Yet even among those thousands I know without a single doubt that I'd pick her out in an instant. I craved her when she haunted my fever delusions like a madman chasing after his sanity. Now that she's gone, I half wish I was back in that state, just to see her again.

What spell did the hag put me under? Why torture me this way?

There is a new girl on my staff. Her name is Jocelyn. Pretty little thing. Shy, too. She never looks me in the eye and blushes every time she has to speak to me. I request her to bring me all my meals while I am forced to bed rest. Her flushing cheeks are the only amusement I have, and I take advantage of it at every opportunity with a sly remark here and a mild innuendo there. It doesn't take much, really.

When I am strong enough again, I make my way down to the library. I instructed Jacques to have new books brought in and he delivered two hundred new volumes, which undoubtedly cost a fortune. Happily, I have several to spend and the expense is trifling. I peruse the newly filled shelves for something to catch my interest. There is the usual intellectual bore, the dense classics.

Then my gaze snatches on a volume of folk tales. It's hand penned like a journal, by an author whose name I do not recognize. I take it with me to the settee and force my eyes to cooperate and read a few pages. Before long I have a splitting headache and my eyes are closing of their own accord. I curse and hurl the book.

I almost hit Jocelyn and her food tray. "I-I'm sorry, my Lord," she stutters.

"What is the point of this fucking library if I can't even read?" I snarl.

Jocelyn blushes fiercely at the profanity. She sets the tray down on a table and retrieves the book, smoothing the covers. Her eyes flit briefly to me before she drops her gaze again. This is interesting.

"Read it to me," I command.

"I... I..."

"You can read, can't you?"

"Y-yes, my Lord. A little."

Frustrated beyond belief, I huff at her. "Raise your head, child. You'll get a hump in your neck. I'm up here, not at your feet."

"Yes, my Lord," she says. Her gaze stays on the floor.

I roll my eyes. "Read."

She opens the book. "H-han-sel and Gret-tel." Jocelyn reads slowly, with the unease of one not familiar with the written word. I can see from the way she is near tears that her illiteracy embarrasses her.

"Stop," I say, taking pity on the girl.

She falls silent with a sigh of relief.

"I want you to learn to read," I tell her. When her wide, hopeful eyes lock with mine, I shift uncomfortably. "When you have free time, you will come here and read aloud until you can finish a sentence without stumbling over the words, understand?"

She nods jerkily. "Yes, my Lord." She looks much too happy for a woman who hasn't just climaxed.

"Take the book and go." I've lost my taste for it. And her.

She curtsies and leaves.

It's another week before I'm back to myself, and by then I am going out of my mind, trapped inside my own castle. Night after night I have to stop myself from riding out to that shack again. It's not Lilith that pulls me there, but the hag. I need answers only she can give me. But I know now the moment I am close to the Faery court, the black cup will be beckoning just like last time.

I'm not an idiot. Thinking back on that night I recognize what I hadn't then. Lilith and her court are fly traps for humans. They lure us mortals into their world to amuse them, use their magics to make us think we have a choice.

We don't. To the Faery folk we are no more than insects, and they ever delight in tearing off our wings and making us whole to do it all over again. A stronger, wiser man would stay far away from that place.

But there is something in those mystical woods I want, a question I need answered and before the week is out, I can no longer contain myself. I inform Jacques that I am leaving and not to expect me for a while. If he has an opinion, he keeps it to himself. I ride through the chill evening and arrive at the hag's table just as the sun dips behind the mountains.

She lights a torch and turns a card. Judgment.

I don't have my own deck with me. Instead, I reach for hers and take the top card. I don't expect it to be relevant. To my surprise, it is The Moon. The same moon I see in my dreams each time I drink from the white cup. The same wolf on a cliff, howling at it.

She takes the next card. The Tower. I frown at the face of it. It looks uncannily like my castle, the balcony of my chambers lit from the inside and a shadowed figure standing at the balustrade. Is she telling me to go back?

I should. Already my attention is more on the curtained door behind her than on what she is telling me. There must be a compromise here, some middle ground. Perhaps I was too exhausted last time to dream of my Strength. If I just pace myself this time, maybe I can find her. I need to know who she is, whether she's real or simply a figment of the hag's meddlesome spell.

I turn my card without looking and the hag sighs. Temperance? I pulled Temperance?

As if she has given up on me, she fans the deck and pulls out the Five of Pentacles. I scowl as I hand over the coins. The woman is gouging me, I know it. "There," I say. "Buy yourself a better cloak."

I enter directly into the bower, with a black cup already waiting for me. I was expected. "You made me wait, lover," Lilith's disembodied voice croons. Bracing myself with grim determination, I down the contents without once looking at the mirrors.

I don't remember the white cup. My dreams are filled with thorns and not a single bloom. When I awake on the floor of the shack, I know I won't be dreaming the woman again no matter how often I come here and drink the black cup. She's gone. I lost her. No more point in returning here, then. I make that decision before I even have my feet under me. I feel hollow, as if I've lost something precious, a part of myself I never knew I had, and the hole left behind is quickly filling with resentment.

Damn Louis for bringing me here, and damn Lilith for making me this craven for something I never should have had to begin with. I hope the both of them rot in hell.

Outside, it's day time. Frost makes the dry grass crunch beneath my shoes. The hag is not there, but I didn't expect her to be. I look for the rose and instead find a single tarot card.

The Hanged Man.

Chapter Ten

Dreams used to mean little to me. Vague snatches of images, faces I knew or not, voices saying things that made no sense. They were nothing more than the imaginings of a tired mind after a busy day of revelry and drink. Rarely did I wake after a dream and think it had any meaning beyond the immediate.

I was a fool.

Dreams are far more than anyone gives them credit for. I doubt even fortune tellers and mystics know what their dreams are trying to tell them. A tarot card appears on a table. They grasp for meaning based on what they were taught about the card. A King of Pentacles, for example, is supposed to mean a prosperous man with a family and estates. It means wealth, luck, and contentment. A King of Pentacles is what the hag ascribed to me. She called herself the Hierophant.

I wonder if perhaps her deck was stacked.

Not a night goes by now when I do not dream. Dark visions of pain and torment, chains and emptiness. A presence nearby, kept away, out of sight. I call out to it, will it to approach, but it shies away with fear. Every time it does this, I hear a creature howl in agony inside my chest as it dies a little more.

I pour over books on mysticism, superstitions, magic and clairvoyance. I spend hours and days in my library, hardly eating, trying to reason out what it all means. Vague portents of doom are all I find. Any one of the elements in my dreams can be explained by these books, but all of them together make no sense at all. I make myself half insane trying to unravel it, eagerly retiring to my bed each night, waiting to dream something more to help me understand.

I stop hoping for the woman of Strength. She is well and truly gone, not a hint of her left behind, not even her rose. I study the card so much it's worn and fraying. I purchase several more decks, hoping that one of them will hold an image different from the one I have. I find a fist, a warrior, a bulwark, a mighty oak, but no woman. And no rose.

Why would a rose signify strength? Roses are delicate things, finicky about where they grow and how they want to be cared for. They have long stems which break easily, and heavy blooms which weigh them down, making them even more fragile. Their only defense is the thorns.

My garden is empty. On my order, all the plants and flowers were torn out to make room for roses. They are already planted, waiting for spring to bloom into their full glory. I find myself counting the days until the first blossom opens.

I don't like what this obsession has made of me. I've become a hermit, no longer interested in any of my usual sins. When the endless cycle of frustration and fervor is at its worst, I even contemplate seeking out Louis. Perhaps he knows more than I do. Perhaps once I tell him that I am no longer seeing Lilith and he is welcome to her and the damned elixirs, he will settle his feathers and speak to me as a friend once more.

On a sunny winter day, that hope has me mounting my horse and riding into Fauve.

The village is battened down against the cold. People avoid the outdoors most days, but today the sun is warm enough that it lures out the children and with them everyone else. They call greetings as I pass. I wave absently as is my duty, but ignore them for the most part.

Louis' estate is set far enough from the village that he can see the whole of it from his windows. I give my reins to one of his hostlers and knock. There was a time when I would simply enter and seek him out. I'm afraid that time has passed.

The butler opens and ushers me inside. He takes my coat and informs me that Louis is in his study. I find him there, in front of the hearth, with a drink in his hand. "What do you want?" are the first words out of his mouth.

"To talk."

"What is there left to say?"

"That I am sorry?" The apology comes easily because I'm saying it to myself. I am sorry. I regret what I have done, the time I lost to Lilith. I regret it for my own sake, not Louis'.

He probably knows it, too. When he turns to glare at me, it is not with forgiveness or understanding, but accusation and malicious joy. I did this to myself, just as he is the originator of his own misery. He was the one who wanted to boast to me of his conquest and lost it to me instead.

"That you are. A sorrier bastard than you have any right to be."

I wonder whether he's taken a look in the mirror lately. "May I sit?"

He snorts. "Do whatever the hell you want. You're going to, anyway."

I sit. There are things I want to say to him, questions I want to ask, but I don't know how to begin.

"You're staring," he says.

"You should have told me."

Louis laughs. "And would you have believed me?"

He has a point. "Have you been back since ...?"

He shakes his head and takes a drink. "But I can tell you have. Have you enjoyed yourself?"

"Immensely," I retort in the same bitter tone. "What do you know about the hag?"

His glass stops halfway to his mouth. "The hag?"

"The one with the tarot cards."

Louis chuckles and then bursts into laughter. "You saw the Faery court, you made love to their princess, one of the highest, most beautiful beings on this Earth, and you want to know about some hag?"

Lilith is their princess. I vaguely remember the voices in her bower whispering something like that. I never paid much attention. "I think the hag—"

Louis hurls the glass at the hearth. It shatters in the flame, making it flare up higher for just a moment. He shoves to his feet and self-preservation forces me to match him. "She offered me immortality," he snarls in my face. "I was this close to becoming one of them before you waltzed off with her."

He can't possibly have believed her. A creature like Lilith doesn't consort with beings lesser than her except for temporary entertainment. Was Louis in love with her? Blinded by his own foolish emotions, did he swallow every lie she told him?

"I may not have lasted very long, but at least I had her respect," he rants. "You are nothing but her pet. She will tire of you soon enough, and when she does, oh, my dear boy, mark my words, you will rue the day you laid eyes on her."

I already do. "And when she rains down her punishment upon my head," I say dramatically, "will you be satisfied? Will you put this behind us?"

Louis pulls back, surprised out of his anger. "Yes."

I nod. There is nothing left to say, then. I take my leave without another word.

By the time I get back I am in a right foul temper. I stomp past the servants hanging tapestries to ward off winter's chill and head into the library.

Jocelyn is there. She jumps at my entrance and then smiles brightly. "My Lord! I am reading about the Greek gods. Athena, and Zeus, and Eros—"

I stop her mouth with a kiss. She gasps and her hands flutter against my shoulders before curling into my lapels. I pick her up and lay her down on the settee. It takes some creative maneuvering to rearrange her clothing and mine without slipping off the cushions, but then her breasts are finally bared to me and my cock is free of my pants and I am tearing through her maidenhead and silencing her cries with my mouth.

I stroke her pain away slowly, stoke her passion into a fever pitch, and pretend she is the one I want to be holding in my arms. Not a wide eyed maid or a heartless Faery princess. I stroke her black hair and pretend it's red-brown instead. I look at her mouth because her dark eyes are nothing like the blues I crave, and I rock against her, into her, willing my dream into reality.

My powers of will are insufficient, and the shocked squeak she emits when her first orgasm rocks her breaks me out of the bitter fantasy just as I take my own release. Jocelyn is weeping and smiling at the same time. She looks awed, love struck. I break loose of her embrace and hastily rearrange my clothes. Tugging her skirts back down, I leave her to set the rest of her gown to rights and make a hasty retreat to my chambers.

My hands shake when I pour water into the wash bowl. It's frigid cold when I splash it on my face. When I look up, my own haggard, half animal reflection mocks me from the mirror. I tear the silvered glass from its moorings on my dresser and smash it on the floor.

Chapter Eleven

Two months after I left Lilith's bower I've all but forgotten about her. My castle is in quiet uproar over Jocelyn. It seems she hasn't told anyone about me, but the moon eyes and dreamy smiles she wears day after day have betrayed her. Her aunt Aimee especially seems to be in a snit, equally angered with the girl and disappointed with me. As the head of staff, I assign the blame fully on her shoulders. Jocelyn is her niece and her responsibility. If I am such a menace to womankind, Aimee should have warned the girl.

I request my meals to be brought by someone else and avoid Jocelyn as much as I can. The handful of times we cross paths, she smiles at me with some secret knowledge I most definitely do not share and makes me all but run in the other direction. Childish infatuation. It will pass soon, I hope. If I must be more direct with her and explain the exact nature of her status in my castle, it will not go over well. I should hate to have to turn her out.

A snow storm blows in at Christmas time. The roads become impassable and the winds howl through the crenellations, threatening frostbite for any who dare venture outside. Only the most able bodied men go out, and then only to chop more wood. We are fortunate to be surrounded by trees, as we burn through them quite quickly to keep warm.

I spend my idle time in solitude, reading or absently shuffling tarot cards. Christmas itself passes quietly for me. It is tradition here for all the servants to have the day to themselves, and I don't see even one of them from sunup until sunup the next day. At least I can walk my hallways in peace and look forward to a happy, smiling staff when they return. It takes little to make them happy. Most days I simply don't bother.

On the night the storm breaks, I dream of Lilith and wake close to dawn hearing whispers call my name. Somehow my balcony door has come unlatched, letting in the frigid wind. I close it, pull the heavy drapes shut against the morning light, and go back to bed.

I dream Lilith is standing in my chambers, stripping out of her gown and beckoning to me, and when I wake again, I find I've slept through most of the day.

It happens twice more that week and then the hallucinations start. I hear Lilith's voice calling to me on the wind outside, on a stray breeze inside the castle. I see shadows flitting about where there ought not be any, and the face of every woman in my castle begins to resemble the Faery princess in some way.

Just when I think I can't stand it any longer, the bitch herself appears at my doorstep. Dressed as a proper lady, her hair braided in the latest style and a thick fur cloak wrapped around her shoulders, she steps into my entry hall as if she is paying a social call. She has the temerity to smile at me, but her eyes are cold. "Hello, Bastien."

"What are you doing here?"

"My Lady," Jacques says, "would you care for some refreshment? Shall I stoke the fire?"

She waves her hand and the fire flares up, startling my butler half to death if the way his eyes subtly widen is anything to go by. "I have everything I need," she says. "You may go."

Jacques obeys.

"Lover," she purrs when he's gone. "It's been too long."

I grin. "Did you miss me, Lilith?"

Lilith smiles and produces a black flower cup.

My smile wanes in a hurry. "You wasted a trip. Go home."

Shock mingles with anger in an expression I never thought to see on her face. Her eyes quickly morph from human brown to the colorless shine of her natural appearance. It's almost comical the way she gapes, her lips parted the slightest bit with incomprehension. "Go home? Is that all you have to say to me?"

I recall everything I wanted to say to her not so long ago, the accusations, the anger I hoped to unleash on her, fully expecting her to laugh in my face. None of it seems to matter anymore. Lilith is an immortal. In this world she is nothing but a creature of fantasy and myth. In that sense, she might as well not exist. She is nothing to me.

But she is the Faery princess. It occurs to me that if anyone knows about the hag and her magic tricks, it's Lilith. She could tell me whether the woman I saw is real or not. I could charm the answers out of her. God knows she enjoys me enough to seek me out when I don't come to her. It shouldn't be too hard to draw the truth from her lips.

As soon as the idea comes to me, I reject it. Violently. Not once have I mentioned the hag or her cards to Lilith and something, some lingering effect of the tarot spell perhaps, makes me think I shouldn't mention it now. A female's wrath is a thing to be avoided at all cost but strangely it is not for myself that I do this now. "Yes," I answer her shortly. "That is all."

"I am not finished with you!"

For all that she is a Faery princess, seasoned and ancient, she is easily as tenacious as any spoiled human girl I've ever had the bad luck of laying with. Her appeal has already faded. "Go home, Lilith. It's been an enjoyable experience, but it's time to move on. One should always stop before the sweet nectar grows sour, don't you think?"

It's the same thing Madame Bordeaux told me the day she broke off our liaison. She said it the same way, in a soft, tempered tone that made me agree with her. We kissed and parted amicably as friends. I never begrudged her any of her lovers, just as she never became bitter of any of mine.

Lilith's face becomes so pale it glows and realize my mistake. The Faery princess is not human, she's not used to being denied and will most definitely not react in any way I can anticipate. "You think to dismiss *me*?" she hisses.

Before I can formulate an apology, spin a graceful sentence to ease her growing temper, she swirls her cloak and transforms into her true visage, a goddess bright as the sun, her hair flowing about her on currents of magic. The light she casts is terrible. Her voice booms and makes the stone walls shudder.

I fall to my knees and cover my ears as she screams her fury. *"Mortal scum!"* she roars like an avalanche set to bury me alive. *"Heartless monster with a pretty face! We'll see how pretty you are when I show you your true self!"*

Lightning cracks and sizzles all around me, bouncing off the walls. It strikes me down, again and again, battering me from all sides until I am sure I'm about to die.

"I curse you, Beast, and all you posses!"

My body shatters into a thousand pieces, and then those pieces smash back together again. I can't find breath to scream. Blinded by light and darkness in turn, I catch glimpses of my own hands. They are monstrous, clawed appendages that cannot belong to me. I squeeze my eyes shut and just catch a quick flash of a face. Redbrown hair, pale skin, pink lips parted on a gasp, blue eyes wide with fear. My Strength, the woman from my dreams silently shouts my name and then she is gone and I am alone again, dying.

Lilith's voice tears through the lingering memory of her face. *"Find someone to love now, Beast, or stay this way forever!"*

The scream is mine. It's the last of me that exists before it transforms into a terrifying roar and I am no more.

Chapter Twelve

When he wakes he is on the cold stone floor with no notion how he got there, or why every bone in his body hurts so much he can hardly move. Through the pounding in his head he hears sobs. He groans and slowly opens his eyes. There are bright sparks flashing everywhere, making it difficult to focus, but as they begin to fade he can see the fire has gone out. The only illumination comes from candles and torches held by the people around him. Maids, servants, hostlers and cooks, the entire household staff is there, staring and weeping.

None of them come to his aid, so he is forced to struggle to rise on his own. Every move is agony when he is weak and aching like a weathered old man, but at last he makes it to his feet. The women scream, causing needles of pain to stab through his ears and he snarls.

Torches wave back and forth as though to ward him off, and the staff backs away from him with garbled shouts. They are so small he towers over them. It must be some sort of illusion. He must be feverish or injured in the head somehow.

His balance is wavering. He sways and tilts sideways, and before he can catch himself he is falling against an empty suit of armor. It clatters to the floor along with him, the sound piercing his sensitive ears. He roars, startling himself as well as the others. His limbs are tangled in the armor, but he can't fight himself free and falls back to fours more often than not.

Panic begins to sink in. Nothing is working right, not his arms, or his legs. His tail swishes of its own accord, knocking down a candlestick and setting the tatters of his clothes on fire. He tries to cry out and produces something akin to an animal wail. Uncomprehending, terrified, he lashes out at the armor breastplate, sends it flying into what remains of the crowd of servants.

They scatter.

An acrid taste on his tongue has him sneezing. Fear. He is tasting the air, and it's saturated with fear. Desperate to escape, he bounds up the staircase, pieces of armor still threaded onto his limbs. He runs as though a monster is nipping at his heels, and when he slips and collides with the door, it is knocked off its hinges. Nothing to place between him and the beast. He runs into the darkest corner he can find and curls up, making himself as small as possible. Even so, he is larger than the massive bed.

Footsteps rush up the staircase toward him. He is trapped. Cornered. His lips draw back in a feral snarl and a growl reverberates in his massive chest. He doesn't understand what's going on. What happened to him?

The footsteps slow out in the hall. Three men approach with caution whispering to each other. He can scent their apprehension and something else. Something... cold and metallic. Weapons. Without conscious thought, his claws curl downward and snatch on the carpet, ripping into it. He stares down at his own paw. It used to be something else. Something smaller, more delicate. It used to hold things and not destroy them.

"Stop!" someone out there shouts. A fourth man, his voice calm and steady, familiar. "Put those away this instant."

"You saw it! You saw what it did!"

What did it do? What is *it*? Are they talking about him?

"Let me speak to him."

"Are you mad?"

"You can stand guard by the door. If I need assistance I'll call for it. Until then, stay out of sight!"

The man comes inside. His scent is in the anteroom, and then closer. His shadow fills the doorway and stops. "My Lord?" he says in a tempered tone. "My Lord."

The creature in shadow works his tongue around in his mouth. He remembers how he used to use it. Now his mouth feels different. His tongue and throat are strange. "I..." he tries, frightened by his own rumbling voice. But it is a voice. Not a growl, howl, or wail. He can speak. "I am... no lord."

The man in the doorway comes a step closer. "Do you know me? I am Jacques, your head of household."

The name is familiar. He has difficulty saying it. It takes three tries to get his tongue to cooperate. "Jacques," he repeats. "What... am I?"

There is something akin to relief in Jacques' scent. He turns away to wave the others off and they retreat. Another step closer. Too close. At his growl, Jacques stops and lowers to one knee. "Your name is Bastien Sauvage," he says. "You are the master of this castle."

"No!"

Jacques flinches but doesn't retreat. "I know you are afraid. There is no need. We all know you. We know you would not harm us. Please, let us help."

"Can you ... save me?"

Sadness. It weighs heavily on Jacques and the creature, too. "I'm afraid not."

I am a beast. The shining female called him that, so it must be true. His name is Beast. And he cannot be saved. He tears into his chest with sharp claws, throws his massive head back and howls. Far in the distance, in the deep woods that smell of darkness and mystery, a pack of wolves answer his wretched cry.

Chapter Thirteen

Despite Jacques' soft tones and reassurances, the Beast will not be coaxed out of the darkness. He can hear the others far below, arguing, weeping. They are terrified. Half of them want to run and the other half is ready to take up pitchforks and kill the Beast.

Finally, Jacques relents and seeks out the others to tell them what happened. Jacques knows so much that the Beast is sure the man must have seen it happen, for even he doesn't remember some of it. The butler tells them the enchantress cursed them all. They don't believe him.

Jacques sends a young boy to fetch Monsieur Lafarge. More people? Aren't there enough already? The Beast stops listening. He cautiously comes out of hiding and stalks the chamber. It is somehow familiar to him, but he can't be certain he's been here before. It feels like his lair, smells familiar enough, but nothing looks as it should. So much he has forgotten. Jacques called him Bastien.

There is a portrait of a man on the wall with a plaque which reads that name. He is handsome, with golden hair and a smartly cut coat. But his eyes are cold and hard, and the smile on his face is a mocking smirk.

The Beast turns away from it and goes searching for more. He finds clothing tailored to a man, much too small for him, yet the fabrics match the tatters still hanging on his frame. Could they have belonged to him?

The balcony is closed. He fumbles with the latch as gently as he can to open the door. The delicate hook breaks off in his claws, but the door opens and he can step out into the night. From here, he can see the forest surrounding this castle as well as lights in the distance, a village of some sort.

Fauve. Yes, that is the name of it. The village of Fauve. And he remembers, too, that a Monsieur Lafarge lives on the other side of it. He used to know the man's given name as well. Lars? Louis. That's it. They are friends... or used to be.

Memories flit like ghosts across his mind. They come slowly as the night passes him by. He doesn't want to sleep, too afraid of what he might see in his dreams, but all too soon exhaustion claims him and he is plunged into a life that used to be his.

It's a nightmare. The Beast sees as though through the eyes of another. It must be another; some demon crawled up from the pits of hell. No man could be so cruel and heartless. Yet even as he denies his own past, he knows every detail to be true and it horrifies him.

When he sees the enchantress, a matchless beauty clad in mist, beckoning to him, when he feels his treacherous body respond to her, he wakes with a roar. Blinded with fury, he lashes out at everything in sight. He shreds the bed to pieces with hardly a blink. The armoire breaks apart, the glittering bottles of liquor shatter all around. The Beast tears clothing into ribbons and then sinks his claws into the source of his misery—the portrait. Ripping that smug face off the canvas brings him little satisfaction.

He collapses to the floor, breathing so hard he is growling without meaning to, and sees something red beneath a fall of tattered bedding. It stirs another kind of memory. He pads over to it and with a single claw draws out a card. It is a rose, with the word Strength written above it.

"Well, my boy. It would seem I was right."

The Beast turns his head toward the voice. He didn't hear the man enter, yet there he is. Louis Lafarge, his once oldest friend. His eyes are wide as he beholds what the Beast has become, but he does not fear. The Beast slides the Strength card back out of sight. "Have you come to gloat?"

"I don't think that's necessary, do you?"

The Beast growls.

"Come on, then, let's see what we can do to make you more presentable."

The bathing room is attached to these chambers, just off the anteroom. There are mirrors in there so large the Beast can see the whole of himself. "I am a monster," he says.

His bulk is easily twice as big as any man. His jaws could crush a skull with ease. He has a short snout, but massive fangs. A lion's mane, but the torso of an animal used to throwing its weight around. His front paws have an almost opposable thumb—he can grasp things, but with difficulty—and his claws don't retract. His hind legs and paws are just wide enough that he can stand on twos, but his sheer size makes that the least favorable position. There is a tail, too. Not short, nor long, somewhere between a panther and a fox. The wicked Faery has turned him into a mismatched puzzle of animal parts covered in golden fur, with just enough humanity to make him the stuff of nightmares.

"Yes, you are," Louis says. "Some might say you always were."

The Beast drops his gaze.

"Will you tell me what's happened? Do you even remember? Jacques seems to think your memory was affected by the spell."

"I remember," the Beast says. But he doesn't tell. Caution keeps him silent; he doesn't want Louis to know about the rose.

"Very well, then." Louis calls for servants to bring hot water and a tailor to clothe the Beast. He remains in the room while they work, an unspoken assurance that the overlarge monster is harmless. They still fear him. They can see what he did to his own chambers.

Jacques is there, too. He tells Louis about the spell, that all of the castle and its inhabitants are affected by it. He says several servants have tried to leave already but were somehow... prevented from crossing the gates.

"But the boy got through," Louis says.

"It would appear so," Jacques replies.

"The boy returned," the Beast says. "The others would not have."

"Could it really be that simple?" Jacques asks.

"Despicably simple, if it's true. A clever little spell," Louis says. "You can leave so long as you intend to return. If not, you are bound to the castle grounds. A lovely gilded chain she put on the lot of you."

"What if one leaves with the intention of returning and somewhere along the way changes his mind?" Jacques muses.

Louis shrugs. "I would imagine in such a case the curse would somehow compel him to come back." He chuckles. "The cruelty of it is... almost fitting."

The Beast hangs his head. He can't look at them anymore. Because of his mistakes, and everything else he did with calculated intent, everyone in this castle must suffer with him.

"Except it's not, is it?" Louis says, watching him closely. "Bastien, tell me about the last woman you fucked."

The Beast snarls at him. "What your tongue!"

Louis' eyes grow wide again. "Bastien would have told me. He would have boasted and described every last detail." He exhales a breath of stunned wonder. "Sweet God above, it's not you at all."

Chapter Fourteen

The servants decide the only way to break the curse is to kill the Beast. It only takes them a week to rack up their courage. They chase him out of the castle and into the snowy garden. He is more certain out of doors. In the middle of the garden he turns on them and roars at the top of his massive lungs. Those at the front of the mob fall back and one man impales himself on a spear.

All of them stop in shock and horror. They watch the spear be pulled from the dying man, watch his blood soak the snow, and do nothing as he gasps for breath. Then he stops breathing all together.

"You monster!" a woman screams at the Beast. She throws a rock at him. More follow, trying to chase him off. They throw anything they can get their hands on—his own people trying so hard to kill him without getting too close to his fangs.

A large rock strikes his head, drawing blood. A pitchfork embeds itself in his hide, just deep enough to stick. He barely moves in time to avoid a spear aimed directly at his heart. The Beast roars again, hoping to frighten them away but the assault continues, edging him farther from the castle and he can do nothing without harming them.

He's about to run for the woods when one man shouts, "Wait!" It's loud enough to make all of them stop. "Look!" He's crouched next to the fallen servant. Before their very eyes, the dead man breathes a sigh and sits up, rubbing his chest. It's miraculously whole and unharmed.

Not a sound comes from the stunned mob that just moments ago nearly drove the Beast into the woods for good. Not one of them sees or cares when he pulls the pitchfork out of his hide and retreats into the castle.

This is how the inhabitants of the Beast's castle discover that one affected by the curse cannot break it. It means he can't even kill himself to be free of it. Lilith said, "Find someone to love now, Beast, or stay this way forever." Apparently, forever would be too short a time if one was allowed to die. The Faery princess gave the Beast and all his servants the one thing Louis coveted so much. Immortality.

Now, as evening turns to night, Jacques is the one who brings the Beast supper. The others, though resigned to their fate, refuse to come near him.

At least he doesn't have to suffer the indignity of having them see his struggles to feed himself. It is difficult for the Beast to grasp utensils. He drinks his soup and eats meat and potatoes with his bare claws.

The two speak little while the Beast eats. Then Jacques says, "The others will come around."

"You said that before. What will they bring next? Axes and bows? Hunting dogs?"

"They're scared. Rightly so. Because of your... because of the Lord's carelessness they are trapped in here, quite possibly forever."

"As am I," he growls irritably, but immediately ducks his head in shame. "I didn't mean ..."

Jacques waves the comment aside. "It's obvious that only love will break the spell. And you can't be seen outside, so the solution is perfectly clear. We must help you."

The Beast laughs.

"If we want to be free—"

"What do you suggest? Will you be sending errand boys to Fauve to fetch me young maidens to terrify? There isn't a woman alive who wouldn't run screaming at the sight of me."

"You must have hope, Master."

"I told you not to call me that."

"As I recall, you said not to call you Lord. You are not Bastien and I will not call you Beast, Master."

The Beast scowls but can think of nothing to counter that. "Hope," he says instead, thinking of the rose. There is something about it he's forgetting. "Yes, just enough to torment me for the rest of ever."

Jacques clears the empty tray. "If that is what you wish to believe, Master. In my humble opinion, a monster's visage over a good heart is always better than a pretty face with no heart at all." By the door, he pauses. "The Lord wondered once why the servants were so cold. It's not because of the man he was. It's because we knew the man he could be. I believe I see that man in you now. The others will too, soon enough."

The Beast huffs.

"Then again," Jacques add, "the moon is full tomorrow night. Perhaps we shall see another side of you all together." Despite his good natured smile, his words send a chill up the Beast's spine. He rushes to the windows to seek the moon. Sure enough, only a minuscule sliver of shadow obscures its round face.

The Beast doesn't sleep a wink that night.

As soon as morning dawns, he goes in search of the servants. Many cower at the sight of him. He has to corner three of them and growl them into silence for them to listen to his demands.

"Bring me chains," he says. "As thick as you can find, as many as you can spare or buy."

"Master," one of them says, "is something the matter?"

He doesn't know, but a deep sense of foreboding makes him restless throughout the day.

Jacques watches him curiously as he paces the gardens in the snow. The Beast shakes himself off every once in a while, but the flakes stick to his fur too well. Five men lug chains into the castle, up the stairs to his chambers. There's not enough time to secure them to the wall. He must hope that there are enough, heavy enough to restrain him, should he somehow lose control of himself.

Terrible visions of blood and bodies torn apart haunt him until supper time. He has no stomach for what's on his plate and sends it back with his apologies. The servants are made even more nervous. They're already locked in their rooms, no doubt barricaded in to be safe. If they could leave, they would.

Only Jacques seems unconcerned by any of this. He goes about his duties as if this is just another day and nothing is out of the ordinary. While the Beast watches the sun dip lower with every minute, Jacques hums a tune to himself as he arranges the horse combs on the new armoire.

When he cannot wait any longer, the Beast loops the chains around himself as best he can. They are so tangled and convoluted he will need help getting out of them come morning, but hopefully they will keep him restrained in the night. Once he's sufficiently weighed down and can't move, he asks Jacques to add more.

With a shake of his head, the man obeys, and then sits in an armchair, tapping his foot in a merry rhythm as the sun sets.

For a few moments, the sky retains some of its luminescence. Then even that is gone. Jacques smiles. He opens his mouth to say something when a horrible wail splits the air.

The Beast roars, his body crushing in on itself, tearing apart and growing back together, smaller, so small he can't breathe. His head feels as though it's exploding. Somewhere in the back of his mind he can hear himself screaming for help. He can see flashes of Jacques staring at him in horror. *Run!* he wants to tell the man but can't form the word. Death, that eyeless skull draped in a black, hooded cape, wraps its hands around the Beast's throat. He is dying.

Then everything stops.

Incessant ringing echoes all around in the absolute darkness. One eye opens, then the other. The chains are crushing, but they are loose, easy to slip out of. A hand free, then the other. Every muscle aches and twitches, but works.

Wait... hand?

Yes. And one more. And a chest, arms, legs. A face! Laughter rings out loud and clear, so sweet because it is human. "I'm back!"

Chapter Fifteen

"My... my Lord?"

I laugh at the look on Jacques' face. "So much for the Faery curse, eh?" My joyous bellow echoes in the chamber. I feel so alive my lungs are bursting. I strip out of the clothes too big for me and search for my old things while my butler stares. "What happened to my goddamn wardrobe?" All I find is a worn pair of brown breeches and a torn peasant shirt. I can't think of why I would even own things like this unless it was for some lurid masquerade, but they will have to do. I don't require the height of fashion, just something that will keep me decently covered until I take it off again.

Why is Jacques so quiet?

"Have you gone deaf? I asked you a question."

The man pales.

"Speak!"

Jacques pulls back his shoulders and puts on his most stern face. "I believe your clothes were destroyed... *my Lord*."

"Have them fixed. Better yet, I want new everything." Luckily it seems my boots survived whatever tantrum took place here. I shove my feet into them, impatient to be out of here.

"Are you going out, my Lord?"

I pause at the door. Why is he saying my name that way? "Is that any of your business?" I am alive, I am free, and I am about to overindulge in every vice known to man.

Jacques stands even straighter. "No, my Lord."

I take three steps back to him and lift him by his lapels. "Then the next time you feel the urge to ask," I say, nose to nose with him, "don't."

"Yes, my Lord," Jacques says stiffly. There is that tone again.

I release him with a shove and run down the stairs, straight to the stables. I mount my horse bareback and ride out hard in Louis' direction. The night is rife for sin of the sweetest kind and there is no one I would rather drag into it with me than Louis Lafarge.

I almost break down his door in my haste. He almost knocks over his dinner table at the sight of me. I laugh at the look on his face. "What are you doing dining here alone?" I ask.

"Bastien? How...?"

I grasp his shoulders and shake him. "The night is young, and I am hungry. So stop dawdling and let's go!"

He fires questions at me which I have no intention of answering. I don't care. I don't care what happened to the Beast, or how I came to be myself again. I don't care what the mopey bastard did since Lilith's curse. I only care that I am free and the cold is biting. I ride straight to the brothel and spill a pouch of coin into the purveyor's lap.

A patron objects when I pluck his entertainer from his lap, but I silence him with a quick clip on the jaw. "You," I drawl to the woman with a lusty grin. I look around the chamber, heartily amused at the shocked expressions on each and every face, and point out my selection. "You, and you. Oh, most definitely you." Free or not, all of the women stop what they're doing and come to me. It must be the bulge of my pants luring them. Within moments Louis and I are surrounded by drink and women eager to warm us from the cold.

I drink deep and fuck hard until my body is heavy with pleasurable exhaustion. Multiple sets of hands roam over me. Tongues lave at me, mouths suck on me, and I laugh at the absolute rightness of it all. I am back, and more alive than ever.

Faces hover before me, one more beautiful than the next. I fuck them all, take my pleasure with each of them. I have energy to spare and happily spend it here along with my coin. When one begins to bore me, I take another. Two, three at a time. Laughter and moans are the music of the night, the perfect rhythm to move to. They sigh my name, pour wine into my mouth, onto my cock.

This is beauty—perfect because it is flawed. Cheeks too bright, lips too red, but flesh so hot it burns me and I adore it. The next one who mounts me is stunningly garish in a bright red wig and her clothes dark and stained. I rip them off her and bury my face between her ample breasts as she slams down on me with a slap of flesh against flesh. I lick, she moans. I nip, she screams and clutches my hair. She pulls my head back to kiss me and I frown.

Her skin is suddenly pure as milk, her lips pink and lush. Her eyes, before so dark, now flash blue fire, and her hair is a shade I know all too well.

I shove her off me and snarl. My heart beats too hard, and I shake my head and clutch my temples, blinking past the drunken stupor. The woman is on the floor, scrambling to her feet. "Get out," I snarl.

Garish red hair, painted lips, flushed, freckled skin. Strength is gone again. The whore runs out of the room, weeping. I look at the other, startled female faces. Not one of them resembled the phantom before. Now they all look exactly like her, all staring at me with contempt.

I blink and the illusion is gone, and I am back in the whore house, surrounded by naked flesh.

A burly man with a club in hand stomps in on my celebration. "I knew you'd be trouble," he says, knuckles turning white as his face reddens. In an instant my women are flattened against the walls. I roll my eyes and get out of bed. "You'll regret this," I tell him. "Last chance to—"

He charges with a shout.

I have no other recourse but to fight back. I'm furious that this pile of warthog shit dared to intrude on my revelry, but the fight lights my blood on fire. I break his arm to get the club and then beat him with it until he's a whimpering puddle of piss and misery on the floor. When I grow tired of it I drag the pathetic imbecile out and return to my harem, feeling like a knight who just slew the dragon. I grin hungrily and lick my teeth. "Who's next?"

Half of them run out. The other half compose themselves as best they can and edge closer. Coin is ever the draw, but for their courage I am prepared to pay them a premium not only in gold but in pleasure. The hunger in their eyes may not be for me, but it's enough to keep them here. I'm not particular enough to care why they don't run, only that they stay and do what I pay them to.

When I recline on the bed again, a lushly rounded blond crawls over me, nearly smothers me in her cleavage. I make a note to reward her for it while I reach for the brunette with my right hand and the exotic Gypsy girl with my left. Both of them arch to my fingers and I am a god once again.

By the time the night is through I can scarcely move. Four women are asleep, draped over me and each other. My sigh feels like a benediction to depravity. *Dear God*, I think, *Forgive me for all the sins of the past, and those I have yet to commit in the future. Because you know I will.* The jealous bastard probably won't forgive, though. I've already resigned myself to the burden I must carry—the bitter envy of every angel in the sky.

It's a satisfying notion. A sign of a life well and truly spent. I close my eyes as the sky begins to lighten, a content smile pulling on my mouth. Just an hour or two, I tell myself. And then I can do it all over again.

It's the pain exploding in my chest that wakes me. I am lifted off the bed as my body breaks and shatters. "Noooo!" I roar, fighting my own demise with everything in me. Demons claw into me from the inside, tearing my soul directly out of my flesh. Fire starts to burn me alive, not the everlasting flames of hell, but the sizzling crack of the Faery's lightning.

I hear women scream all around me, I see them running for the door. I smell blood, taste it in my mouth. I go blind and deaf, and then even the agony of unbecoming is gone and I am, once again, to be no more.

In my final moments of awareness, I see a blurry shape run into the room instead of out of it. Louis' voice is shouting from so far away I cannot make out his words. He reaches for me, then recoils. I close my eyes and die.

Chapter Sixteen

Louis pays off everyone who saw the Beast transform, calls for his carriage and helps return him to the castle and his prison, cloaked in a black curtain. He explains to Jacques everything that happened, sparing no detail.

"I saw you change," Louis says. "My God, how can you stand it?"

The Beast doesn't answer. The transformation is a small enough thing. Wretched agony that lasts only until he dies. He doesn't feel his human counterpart's pain, only his own.

Worse are the memories of all Bastien said and did last night. The savage joy he felt in beating a man unconscious, the soul-deep hunger for food, drink, flesh, pleasure and pain—for life. He drank and whored with abandon, as if his actions have no consequences. He certainly didn't give any thought to the number of bastards he may have sired, or what maladies he may have brought back with him.

And still worse is that somewhere deep inside the Beast envies him that freedom of form and conscience. The shame and guilt of it crush him. He cannot meet anyone's gaze; can hardly drag himself back to his chambers.

Once there, he finds that his wardrobe was changed out and another painting of the handsome monster is hanging in place of the one he defaced. *Can I not be rid of him?* Furious, the Beast tears it apart again, rips all the clothes asunder a second time. He prowls through the castle, destroying anything bearing even the slightest resemblance to Bastien. There are many. The man had dozens of portraits made of himself, statues, busts, even a fountain. The Beast destroys it all.

He doesn't stop his rampage until his curse stops it for him. The moment the sun dips below the trees, he transforms again. The Beast tears at his own flesh, desperate to destroy the demon inside him any way he can, even as the human fights his way back into this world and the life he doesn't deserve.

When he wakes the next morning, he is chained. Jacques and Louis are with him, both looking haggard and tired. "We knocked him out," Louis says. "We didn't know what he would do and rather than take the chance, we chained him."

"How do you feel?" Jacques asks.

The Beast groans in answer.

Louis grins. "I figured you might. Here." He hands the Beast a bowl of water that smells of herbs. Not tea, but a tonic. The Beast drinks every last drop.

"Why did you do it?" he asks. "Bastien is your friend."

"I thought so, too," Louis replies. "When he came to me night before last I was half convinced he was back. I thought it meant he learned his lesson, and I was stunned and furious he broke the curse so quickly. But also glad. I expected him to be different, better." He sighs and shakes his head. "I suppose I expected him to be you."

"So did I," Jacques admits. "But we were wrong."

Louis nods. "He was worse than his old self. The way he spoke and acted... even at his worst I've never seen Bastien like that. So... empty."

Yes, empty is the word. The Beast remembers feeling that void inside, as if no amount of anything could fill it. It consumed Bastien and he didn't even care.

"And," Louis adds, "I've never known him to raise a hand to his own staff. After what Jacques told me, well, we thought it safer to..."

"Thank you," the Beast says. Truly, words are not enough. It seems there is nothing he can do to control what his human half does, but somehow, these two men knew and did precisely what was needed. Is this to be his life now? Beast by day, monster by night?

The idea of it terrifies him. "I fear what I remember feeling," he says softly. "Bastien has no conscience, no restraint. He's already caused harm to another; there is no telling what evil he will commit if he is allowed to roam free." Neither Bastien nor the Beast can leave without the curse returning them, but even within these walls there are people who can be hurt by Bastien.

The Beast won't allow that. If he can't control Bastien, then something or someone else will have to do it for him. He looks at the chains that bound him through the night and alights on an idea. "Tell me, Louis, do you know of a good stonemason?"

Jacques and Louis exchange a glance and get straight to it without question.

That night, the Beast changes again. The next morning, Jacques describes to him how Bastien raged to find himself chained to the wall. The Beast doesn't need reminding. The memories are there, separate from his own but still accessible somehow. It's like remembering a dream, hazy and confusing, but somehow his mind is able to make sense of it.

He knows there should be bruises on his arms from the violent way Bastien pulled on his restraints. He remembers every curse his human self roared at everyone within earshot, the threats that made even the bravest cower far away. Bastien was a mad animal last night, without a single thought that didn't call for blood. The Beast is grateful the chains restrained him, but how long can they hold against such onslaught?

They can't. He racks his brain all day long for some way to ensure Bastien won't break free. He even goes down to the dungeon, but finds it useless. No one has used these cells in decades. The entire place reeks of mold and water, all the metal is rusted and the wooden doors are falling apart. The Beast wouldn't trust a dog not to get out of here, let alone Bastien.

Something else will need to be done.

He chains himself again for the fourth night and posts guards outside the door for good measure, but this time he doesn't transform.

For three weeks he continues to sleep in the binds, with a pair of armed guards standing vigil, but Bastien doesn't rise a single time.

Not until the moon is full, and the Beast has almost convinced himself that he's felt the last of Bastien's malice, does the curse take effect again.

In the morning he finds himself wrapped in chains on the bed. The guards tell him Bastien is stronger than any of them anticipated. In his rage, he managed to tear the chain moorings out of the wall and attack them. They were forced to stop him the only way they could—by stabbing him dead. Just like the unfortunate servant, Bastien woke again in minutes, but by then they'd already restrained him.

The Beast has the chains reinforced and threaded through the wall into the chamber on the other side. He tests them himself and only when he is absolutely certain he cannot break free of them does he allow himself to rest until nightfall.

When he wakes, he is in the entry hall with six burly servants and guards, armed with swords and javelins surrounding him. It's Jacques who tells him what happened, and as he speaks, the Beast remembers.

"The chains held," the butler says tiredly. "It was a woman's folly that let loose the monster Bastien." Jocelyn, in her naivety, got past the guards under the pretense of bringing Bastien supper. She released him from the chains, thinking she would be the one to break his curse, make him better.

The moment he was free, Bastien turned on her. He shoved the girl out onto the balcony and nearly strangled her to death before the guards pried him loose. But his hand on her throat was all that held her safe and without it, she lost her balance and fell over the balustrade to her death.

The Beast howls in agony. The memory is so vivid it's as if she's falling again just outside.

"She lives, Master," Jacques says quickly. "But while the guards were distracted, Bastien made it past them, nearly outside. By then, Aimee and the others had seen the girl plummet and, well, in their anger and grief they mobbed him."

"Beat him right dead," one of the guards adds proudly. "Done what we couldn't, they did. The bastard went down like a felled tree and stayed there." He nods in satisfaction. "Job well done, I say. Job well done."

If the curse hadn't brought Jocelyn back...

The Beast snarls and retreats to his chambers. They didn't tell him the whole of it. Bastien didn't just kill Jocelyn. He taunted her first, groped her and jeered, and her fear of him still lingers in this room. She was terrified of the monster she released, but so hopeful that she could change him she never screamed for help. It was by sheer luck that the guards decided to look in on her. If they hadn't, Jocelyn would have suffered far worse than what she had.

Death is easy. One turn of a card and a man goes from here to gone. Nothing to it but darkness between one breath and the next. What Bastien threatened, what he would have done if the guards hadn't intervened, Jocelyn would never have forgotten.

The Beast certainly never will.

He lifts the chains, almost sensing Bastien still inside them, hovering like a ghost right in front of his face. Disgusted, the Beast drops the chains and turns his back on them to stoke the fire. As it blazes to life, he remembers something else. Something the others couldn't know, because they were so intent on killing Bastien they never heard him through their own screams. "*I wouldn't have,*" he shouted with all the righteous anger of one wrongfully accused. Even the Beast doesn't believe his words.

He gives new orders for the dungeon to be cleaned and repaired. It won't be an easy task, certainly not something they can accomplish overnight, but the Beast makes certain the servants appraise him of the progress often so that the knowledge is fresh in his mind. If he remembers Bastien's thoughts, it stands to reason that Bastien will remember his.

Good. It means he will know that if he transgresses one more time the Beast will take away even the remaining comfort of his own bed chambers and chain him in the black, dank oubliette of the dungeon.

He makes it clear that no one is to enter his chambers on full moon nights for any reason. He gives the key to his restraints to Jacques, and the butler is the only one allowed to know where it's kept.

If Bastien can't be trusted around people, then he will spend the rest of eternity in solitude.

Chapter Seventeen

Three nights of the full moon each month, the Beast transforms into his former self. But he is worse. The worst of his flaws—cruelty, apathy, hunger—are all he seems capable of, all amplified into something that is only human because of the face it wears. The Beast, in turn, seems to bear what few virtues the human used to possess—a conscience and a heart. In his beastly form, these things are, again, much stronger than before.

The servants can see it, too. They fear the human more than the Beast. At each full moon, the Beast has them chain him in his chambers, lock the doors and post sentries just outside of it. No one defies his orders again. They give Bastien a wide berth, leave him to rage, to batter and drive himself to the brink of madness.

The Beast sees it all as though from outside of himself, and it is terrifying to behold Bastien turn downright demonic with fury. But a more frightening thing by far is to remember Bastien claw his way back to sanity after he's lost all notion of what that is. His hatred and despair grow with each night he is forced to be bound alone in his tower chambers.

Living Bastien's night after the fact, the Beast knows when his human side learns that anger only makes the others retreat farther. He changes his strategy and starts calling out for help, cajoling anyone who can hear, inviting them, pleading, and offering bribes. It is the last that nearly works. After months of imprisonment, the guards begin to believe Bastien when he says he can release them. After all, if they are no longer in his employ, if he no longer owns them, the curse should set them free. He promises to do this—because the Beast cannot—if only they will set him free.

Twice the guards come close to breaking Bastien's chains. The first time, one stops the other before he steps into Bastien's chamber. The second time, Bastien lures him nearly close enough to set him free, but his eyes betray him. The guard says as much before he runs out, just in time to escape Bastien's wrath.

The Beast doesn't begrudge the guard his desire to be free, but not willing to risk the safety of the others, he has the man removed to another post.

Sunset becomes their witching hour, a time everyone dreads because of what it will surely bring. When dawn breaks each morning, the servants bring the Beast food and clothes, speak to him and give what comfort they can—considerations they cannot and will not offer their human lord.

Louis visits often, though never again on the nights around the full moon. He is true to his word and remains a friend when all others would have abandoned him.

The Beast could not ask for a better friend.

Jacques and Louis devise a plan by which they hope to free the Beast. They are so confident it will work that the Beast doesn't have the heart to tell them how laughable it is. The strategy consists of Louis courting young women in the Beast's stead, telling them just enough of his good qualities to get one to the castle, at which point they expect to tell her the whole truth and hope for the best.

"Even with your title and riches it will take time to earn their trust," Louis warns. "Don't expect a bevy at your door within the week."

"Time we have," Jacques tells him. "Plenty of it."

Time is all the Beast and his castle have.

But not Louis.

At first it is a quest to redeem Bastien's soul. Then it becomes a game. Before long, it begins to take its toll on Louis and everyone else. He no longer laughs when he speaks of the women he met, doesn't tell the Beast to keep his chin up anymore.

His visits become less frequent, and more often than not he avoids talk of women all together. There was a time when he and Bastien talked of nothing else. Now the subject is simply not brought up.

They are failing.

Rumors have spread quickly about a monster inside the castle. No one can tell if they're true, but the threat is enough that not a single person will come near the Beast's lands. Louis tells the Beast that in Fauve they use the threat of him to make their children behave. Whatever hope he's managed to hold on to begins to wither. *Find someone to love, or stay this way forever.* Lilith's words haunt him day and night.

It's useless. Everything they do is for nothing. How could anyone love a creature like him?

A year passes by, and one day Louis comes to tell the Beast he is engaged to be married. He speaks of his fiancé with so much affection, not at all the way he spoke of the Faery princess he was so smitten with. In two months they are wed. In ten more, their first child is born, and the year after that another.

Louis has a family. He is happy. He still visits, though not as often anymore. The Beast envies him bitterly. He shares his friend's joy, in whatever capacity he can, but to see that easy smile on Louis' face only reminds him of his own lonely misery.

Time begins to move differently for him. Before long, Louis is an old man, a widower, his children grown. Hearing stories of his life brings little solace to the Beast and his people, none of whom have aged or changed at all.

One day, his old friend limps in from the cold of autumn, supported by a cane on one side and his eldest son on the other. The Beast watches them from the shadows. "I wish to see him," Louis says to Jacques.

"Do you think that is wise?" the butler asks.

"It is..." Louis coughs and leans harder on his son. "Imperative."

Jacques bows and comes to fetch the Beast.

"No," he growls. "Send them away."

Before Jacques can answer, Louis calls from the entry hall. "Beast! You furry bastard, get down here. I want to... introduce you. To my son." He has to sit when his legs will no longer support him.

The Beast relents and stalks down the staircase, keeping to the shadows. There must be some reason why Louis would expose him this way when he's kept his secret for all these years.

"Ah, there you are. Don't be afraid, my boy," he says weakly. "He wouldn't harm a hair on your head. Isn't that right, old friend?"

The Beast bares a fang. The threat is feeble. He can scent sickness and decay. It's overwhelming. With a low whine, he nudges Louis, mindful of his fragile bones. "What ails you, old friend?"

"I am dying," Louis says with a tired smile, then scowls. "Now don't you fuss. I've lived a good life and I regret very little." Their eyes meet in silent communication. Some things a father is compelled to share with his progeny, but some secrets a friend can never speak of.

The Beast nods in understanding.

"It's time I put my affairs in order. And how could I leave you in this world all alone?" He looks up proudly at the young man standing next to him. As well he should. His son is scared, that much is obvious, but he doesn't move from his father's side. He stands his ground straight and proud, much the same way Louis used to in his youth. They are alike, but beneath the similarities and the fear in the boy's eyes there is something else—a quiet strength and honor Louis didn't always possess. This is not a man who would take his burdens lightly. He would never say a careless word or perform a thoughtless act.

And unlike his father, he would never do something so foolish as to step foot into the Faery court given a choice. Louis raised him well. So what promise did he drag out of the boy to get him here?

"This is my son, Reinard. He will look in on you when I am gone, won't you boy?"

"Yes, father," Reinard says obediently and there is such gravity in his tone he may as well have taken a blood oath by saying the words.

"Reinard, this is Bastien Sauvage III, Duke of Colline. He is a prince, you know."

The Beast huffs and nods his head.

"You wanted to know my secret, son," Louis slurs. "Here he is. And now... he is your secret to keep." His heart slows, slows, and then stops. Louis' eyes close.

"Father? Father!"

He will not wake.

As Reinard sinks to his knees in grief, the Beast howls his own.

Chapter Eighteen

Reinard is a good, steadfast man. He becomes as much a friend to the Beast as his father was. But this, too, doesn't last. Soon it is Reinard who is married, Reinard who introduces his son to the Beast. The Beast becomes a Lafarge family secret, and for five generations son after son becomes the family he never had.

The solace they bring is fleeting. With each year gone, the Beast comes to realize that there will never be a woman he could ever meet, let alone love. The young Jocelyn—young only in appearance now, as they all are—keeps trying to persuade him the curse can be broken. The right woman is just waiting for him to claim her. Every time she says this, the Beast knows she speaks of herself. He orders Aimee to make doubly sure the girl stays away from the west wing all together, especially on full moon nights. The last thing they all need is for her to foolishly enter his chambers again when Bastien is in residence.

As the seasons change, so does his curse. The Beast finds he not only remembers what Bastien did or thought on the nights he is free, he is sometimes present enough to see for himself. And in idle times during some days, he can feel his human half wake inside him for brief moments. It never lasts long, but in those episodes the Beast can feel Bastien's resentment, bordering on madness. It is perhaps cruel to keep him chained, but even when he is quiet behind closed doors no one will trust him enough to release him for even an hour, and he has done nothing to persuade them otherwise. If anything, the curses and threats he still sometimes screams in fits of madness make everyone even more determined to keep him contained.

To ease some of the torment, the Beast stocks his bed chamber with books.

Year after year, decade after decade this goes on, an unchanging routine in their ever constant lives. Beast for a month, monster for three nights of it.

Until one day, Jean Lafarge, the sixth generation son and only heir to the Lafarge name walks in the door.

He is not like his predecessors. Where they have been cautious, respectful, even brotherly, Jean is more reserved and distant. Of all the men of his family, he reminds the Beast most of Bastien. That same emptiness lurks in his eyes, the same skewed smirk creases his face when he deigns to smile. To him, the Beast as an obligation and he makes it clear with look and gesture if, not with words, that this obligation is not a welcome one.

The Beast has resigned himself to Jean being the last human he will see in his eternal misery. He endures the strained visits for the sole purpose of learning about the world. Where his servants can go to Fauve for short hours, no one has yet managed to step one foot beyond its borders and if they linger past sunset, the curse inexplicably forces them to return. Jean, on the other hand, can go where he pleases. He spends much of his time at court and can tell the Beast more about the changing times than anyone else.

Of course, such answers always have to be pulled from him and it seems he takes great delight in making the Beast wait for them. He enjoys pulling the monster's tail, knowing he will never feel its bite.

The Beast begins to treasure his solitude.

And then, on a sunny summer day, Jean comes in with his young wife on his arm.

"My Lord Beast, may I present Madame Angelique Lafarge."

The Beast bows as properly as he is able while casting a hard glare at Jean. Bastien is stirring inside him, taking an unsettling interest in what is happening.

Angelique curtsies. "My Lord," she says and deep inside the Beast's psyche, Bastien preens.

"The Beast is cursed, Angelique," Jean says in a tone that makes the Beast bristle. "He is a man trapped in the body of a monster. Only under the light of the full moon can he be himself again."

The Beast growls a warning.

Jean turns Angelique to him and says as he would to a child, "You must never come here alone, my dear. And never when the moon is full." He may as well have dangled a sweet before her and told her not to reach for it.

Angelique's eyes grow wide with fascination and she is staring at the Beast when she nods. "Yes, husband."

Jean pats her on the head. "There's my good girl," he says and the Beast wonders whether she is simple in some way, or whether he is simply being cruel. He doesn't object when Jean takes her for a stroll in the rose garden.

"Peculiar one, isn't he?" Jacques says when they are out of earshot.

"Something's not right," the Beast replies. "Keep an eye on them. Make sure they don't stray where they're not supposed to."

"Yes, Master," Jacques says.

But they don't stray. Jean takes Angelique around the garden, brings blooms to her face so she can smell them. He does not cut any, he knows better than to dare. He points out the towers, the architectural details of the castle, the pristinely manicured lawns and many other things which his young wife has no interest in, if the way her gaze keeps straying to the library window and the Beast standing behind it is anything to go by.

The charade is done with soon enough. They come back inside, and Jean lets Angelique get in the carriage first while he collects his hat.

"Why did you bring her," The Beast asks.

Jean smiles, that same skewed smirk. "I thought you'd be happy. My father and grandfather told me so much about you I feel as though we're family. But they never brought their wives or daughters here, did they? I should think it would ease your solitude to have a female visit from time to time. I wonder why they would deny you."

Yes, he is very much like Bastien, seizing on any opportunity to show off what he has to all who don't. He brought Angelique here to show the Beast what he will never have, and for no other reason. His eyes are like mirrors and in them the Beast sees himself, a desolate monster caged in his own castle, with enough coin to buy anything he wants, except the one thing he'll never find. Love.

"Be careful, Jean," the Beast tells him. "Be very careful what you lord over me. You might come to regret it." It's the Beast's voice, but Bastien's words. Taken aback by what he said as much as the look of thinly veiled triumph in Jean's eyes, the Beast shakes himself and retreats to his chambers.

Troubled thoughts send him into troubled dreams that night. He sees memories of visions from centuries ago, things he hasn't thought about in so long they seem figments of his imagination. A painted world from a hag's tarot cards, a wolf howling at the full round moon, a dark cape swirling around a blood red rose...

... and a woman with red-brown hair and brave blue eyes.

Chapter Nineteen

The moon is full. I can tell by the fact that I am human and chained like an animal next to my own goddamned bed. I sit against the wall in the dark and gaze out the open window at the black night sky. The moon's glow is barely visible through the clouds. Everything is so dark my eyes strain to make out the barest hint of shadows.

I was quiet last night, so Jacques decided to call off the guards at my door tonight. He does that sometimes. They're not really necessary anymore. Not when the chains that keep me confined to my bed chamber are as thick as my wrist and anchored so deep in stone even the simpering brooder can't break them. But they like to remind me every so often that, should I attempt an escape, I will not get far.

They will kill me dead on sight, with the happy knowledge that my curse will bring me right back to life in a matter of minutes. Just enough time for them to drag me down to the dungeon, chain me up again and search out the keys I managed to get off of some naive soul or another. I would never see the light of night again.

So here I am, in the dark, with nothing to do. God, I've never been so bored in my life. Well, a man has to entertain himself as he will. I haven't fucked a woman in nine thousand days, not counting the ones when I'm not... here. That's over twenty four years without a slick, warm cunt stuck on my cock.

My pants, or rather, the brooder's pants, because he rips through all of mine when I change into him, are already pooled around my lap and my ballocks are so heavy I keep shifting in place to relieve the pressure. Out of patience, and finding no good reason why not, I shove the pants lower and grab the source of my troubles by the base.

The pride and joy of any man as well endowed as I am. God's most magnificent creation. Woman was an afterthought so man would have something to stick it into.

My vault of memories is extensive, but when I close my eyes, it is my imagination that paints pictures for me in my mind. One fair haired menace in particular, with lips full and plump and breasts just enough to fill my palms. The lovely young Madame Lafarge.

I stroke myself, imagining her mouth on me, cupping my balls and taking me so deep she cannot breathe. Her tongue would be wicked. There are two kinds of women—those who use their tongues to speak, and those who use it for something else. Angelique is definitely the latter. I would wrap her hair around my fist and guide her mouth exactly as I want it, and she would look at me the entire time and say, "Yes, my Lord," to anything I told her to do.

A small gasp in the darkness makes my eyes open. The door is ajar and light filters into the anteroom. Not enough to see details, but enough that I know I am not alone. The Beast's senses sometimes carry over to my human form. Curious if this is one of those times, I inhale deeply and I grin, recognizing the scent of female arousal. It is not anyone of my household that stands just behind my doorway, watching me pleasure myself.

"Come here," I say.

Silence.

"Do you like what you see?"

A blond head peeks from around the door frame and I grin wider. That little minx. How in the hell did she manage to get to the castle, let alone inside and up to my chambers? "Good evening, Angelique." My cock twitches in my hand. I give it another stroke to settle it. "Come closer."

Hesitantly, she steps into my chamber. "It's true," she says. "You really are cursed."

I laugh. "Does this look like a curse?"

She stares at my cock and licks her lips.

"What did you come here for?"

"I... I don't know."

"Yes you do," I counter. "Tell me."

"Why?"

"Because I won't give it to you unless you ask."

She is silent for so long, I get bored and resume stroking myself. At least with her in the room it is easier to imagine her naked and at my command.

Angelique gasps, not only to see me do this, but to see me do it while watching her. "Jean doesn't... he doesn't..."

I roll my eyes at her feeble attempts to explain. "He doesn't make you come. Yes, I gathered. Close the door, child and get in here."

The door shuts and there is darkness again. I hear the hiss of fabric as she disrobes and then she is before me in nothing but a soft blouse, staring at me. I bite back another laugh at her eagerness, spread my knees and let her crawl into my lap. Her woman's juices have already soaked her and she slides so easily onto me my eyes roll back in my head.

She is shivering, holding on to my shoulders, waiting. For fucking what? "Move," I growl grabbing her arse and lifting her up and down over me. Faster, harder. Until she is moaning so loud I'm afraid someone will hear. I shove to my feet and press her against the wall, covering her mouth as I drive into her. She turns hot and pliant in my arms, lost to what I do to her, left completely to my mercy.

She ought to know I have none. When she starts screaming against my hand, I hate her for coming so soon. Her climax forces one from me, but just as I am about to spill inside her, the furry bastard roars inside my head and I pull out at the last second. Even without the feel of her squeezing my seed out of me, it's the best orgasm I've had in centuries.

I fuck her twice more before I send her out with instructions to use the servants' staircase and return in a month. The evidence of

my pleasure I leave for the Beast to savor when he rises. In approx-
imately three minutes.

·

Chapter Twenty

She comes to me twice more, stealing in by the dark of night, always only on the peak of the full moon. I have one night to anticipate and another to savor, and then a month to wait until she shows her face again. I teach her to like things I like, knowing that she will never again be satisfied with her own cold marriage bed. I teach her to crave me more than air, condition her body so that every time she looks at my castle through her window, it weeps for me to fuck it. I am a very efficient tutor.

The Beast is furious. Despite his attempts to thwart her, Angelique keeps getting through his countermeasures and finding my cock by the light of the full moon. He likes to lie to himself, play the righteous one, but we both know better. If he really wanted Angelique to stay away, she wouldn't get past the drive. No, he wants her here as much as I do. It's the only way he can ever feel a woman's heat.

The night grows late and Angelique still hasn't shown herself. I begin to get restless, pacing back and forth between the hearth and the balcony. Where is she? I watch the moon travel across the sky, counting minutes, then hours. I snap my chains, hating them more than I ever have now that they're keeping me from seeking out what I want.

If I want Angelique, I should damn well be able to go after her if she won't come to me. To hell with the Lafarge bastard! I owe him nothing. He is a pretentious prig whose only amusement is the misery of others. If he ever showed himself on a full moon night I would wipe that smug little lip twitch from his face so fast he'd spend the next two hours looking for his teeth all over the floor. What sort of man doesn't even have the sense to bring his wife to orgasm?

From what Angelique told me between gasps, the fool doesn't even try. He comes to his wife's bed each night to rut over her for the sole purpose of begetting an heir. No wonder she seeks her pleasure elsewhere.

As dawn approaches, I begin to worry she will not come. My reasons are purely selfish. If Lafarge discovered his wife is cuckolding him, she will most definitely not show herself here anymore and then I'll be left to my own devices yet again.

Finally I hear footsteps on the staircase. She opens the door and removes her hat in the anteroom, smiles at me as she comes to the door. But she doesn't cross the threshold. "Hello, Bastien," she says. My chains will only let me within two steps of that doorway and she knows it.

"Tease," I accuse. I cannot abide women who lead men around by their cocks and don't even have the courtesy to finish them. "Come say that to my face." I'm already hard for her, as well she can see, since I shrugged out of the Beast's clothes the moment I awoke in anticipation of her arrival. And it's damned cold in here with the balcony open.

"Not tonight," she says. "And not any other night."

I laugh. "We'll see."

"I'm pregnant, Bastien. Jean's seed finally took."

And just like that, my pride and joy turns flaccid. I stare at her belly, trying to see if I can make out any hint of a bulge. "So the bastard finally gets his heir," I mutter. "Have you told him yet?"

"No. I wanted to tell you first. So you would know it's not yours."

"I don't need you to tell me that," I retort. There wasn't a single time I have spilled inside her. Her mouth doesn't count. The child is Lafarge's and most likely took root even before Angelique came to me that first night.

"Obviously I can't keep seeing you."

"Obviously," I repeat dryly, indicating my loins, "I no longer want you to." She couldn't have come up with a more effective way to make herself undesirable.

She smiles a little sadly. "I will... miss you," she says. Already she has that serene, content look on her face, like some fucking Virgin Mary. I've seen it in the eyes of every woman expecting her first child and thanked God every time that I wouldn't have to look at that expression every day for the next nine months or more because the whelp wasn't mine. No doubt she is thinking she has found her calling, her purpose is complete now that she's contributed to the perpetuation of the Lafarge species.

She'll learn otherwise soon enough. An heir always necessitates a spare or two. She'll spend her best years squeezing out Jean's brats until the progeny she has spawned becomes her only appeal. I smile and it feels cruel. "More than you think," I tell her. "Night after night, when you hear your brat screaming from the nursery, when your husband mounts you again for more and leaves you cold and alone in the dark. You will think of me and wish you were in my arms again."

It's unavoidable. She will come to regret taking Lafarge's name but by then it'll be too late. I know all too well that I will see Angelique again. She will come crawling back, begging me to resume our relations, bemoaning her life and expecting me to take pity on her.

And I know it will happen sooner rather than later.

"I expect you're right," she says, the epitome of peace and tranquility. "But when morning dawns again, I will have children to take solace in. You will always have only you."

The chains snap taut and my arms strain to break them. Of course, they will not budge and the stupid bitch doesn't even blink an eye, perfectly safe just two steps away across the threshold. Two steps too far for me to reach across. God, how I want to get my hands on her. Wring her neck and wipe that saintly smile off her face.

I only manage to bloody my wrists in the shackles and the pain is nothing, but that I feel it at all while she stands there watching as if it amuses her makes me livid. "*Get out!*" I roar, so loud I am sure the servants have heard and will be arriving shortly to knock me out.

There's no need. Already the sun is beginning to rise and with it the righteous bastard whom I can hear laughing in my head. As I begin to break apart, I feel Angelique's hand on my face, hear her voice say, "Good-bye, Bastien."

Then she is gone, and so am I.

Chapter Twenty-one

The Beast spends his day in the garden. The last blooms of the season are at their peak. Soon they will need to be cut for the winter and he won't see another rose until next year. He stops at each and every rose bush and takes in their fragrance to keep him through the cold, snowy months. They are remarkably beautiful.

His favorite is the deep crimson, which almost looks black. It grows just outside the library and every time he reads there, he opens all of the windows to let in their scent. There isn't another shade like it. Their scent is different, more potent, and quite unique to his sensitive nose. They also have the sharpest thorns, almost hooked to thwart anyone who would wish to pluck them.

The Beast caresses the delicate petals, soft as velvet to his paw. Beauty never knew a more pleasing form.

The day is cool, but he doesn't mind. He lays in the sunshine, basking in its warmth, however feeble, and feels something akin to contentment. Tonight is the last night of the full moon. One more night in the prison of Bastien's twisted mind, and then he will be free for the next twenty six days. His human counterpart is so furious that, even now, the Beast can feel him.

It makes him smile. Suits him right to be cast aside like a soiled handkerchief. How many women has he left in just this way over the years? It doesn't matter that he never promised them anything beyond a moment's pleasure. The hurt was always there in their eyes and the Beast remembers it well. It's the whole reason Bastien is cursed to begin with.

But thoughts of the Faery princess always sour his mood. He doesn't want her memory spoiling this day.

"The fairs are in Fauve again, Master," Jacques says. "Shall I send the maids?"

The Beast groans. "And have them empty my coffers on frills and ribbons again?"

Jacques chuckles. "One never knows what they might find."

He harrumphs. "Send the driver with them. They are to purchase necessities only. I don't want to have to eat gingerbread for an entire month again because it tasted so good they couldn't resist."

"I shall tell them to take pity on their Master's stomach. They meant well, you know."

He sighs. "They always do."

"Cook has prepared lunch. Will you take it here, or in the dining room?"

"The library." There's a thought. He rises to his paws and meets his butler's gaze. "Tell the driver to bring back more books. Tell the maids the same. They can spend as much coin as they wish, but only on books."

Jacques rolls his eyes. "You have a magnificent library, Master, and your love of knowledge is commendable."

He scowls. "I sense a 'but' coming on."

Jacques spreads his arms in exasperation. "But we have nowhere to put the books anymore!"

The Beast considers this. He pads over to the library window and peers inside. The shelves are filled to bursting and there are stacks of volumes of all shapes and sizes on each table and all over the floor. He backs away and looks up. There is a sitting room above the library which never gets used. Whoever placed it there was an idiot. "Tear out the ceiling," he tells Jacques. "Build up the book cases. Cover all the walls with them, even between the windows." He nods, satisfied with this solution.

Jacques sighs in defeat. "Yes, Master."

And because his staff is fast but not nearly as strong as he is, the Beast spends the rest of the day hauling furniture and stones out of the library. The lot of the household is so busy with the new project no one notices the sun dip low.

"Master," Aimee finally says with deep unease. "The sun."

The Beast nods gravely and throws the stone in his paws outside. He is just passing through the entry hall, on his way to his chambers when he hears a carriage approaching. Frowning, he meets eyes with Jacques, but the butler can only shrug. Company is never expected here. It could only be Jean or Angelique, and it would be too early for her. The Beast is still a beast.

"I can resolve the matter, if you wish," Jacques offers.

The Beast is nodding when the carriage stops and the screaming begins. "What the devil...?"

And a devil it is. The door bursts open and a disheveled Angelique falls in where Jean shoved her. He looks mad, his eyes too bright, his face flushed in anger. He has a pistol in his hand and is breathing hard. Angelique is sobbing and when she pushes herself up to her knees, the Beast can see bruises darkening her face.

His hackles rise. He can already feel the sun setting, the magic which will kill him so Bastien can rise starts to sting. He snarls at Jean as more servants come running to see the commotion. Jacques herds them all back, mindful of the weapon.

"You cheating *whore!*" Jean screams. "Did you think I wouldn't know!" His words run on each other until the Beast can barely understand what he's yelling. Angelique cowers, shielding her belly and the growing child within.

"What is the meaning of this?" the Beast demands.

"*Shut up!*" Jean screams at him. "You shut up! This is all your fault, you and that bastard you turn into. Let him loose!" He levels the gun. "I want him to see this."

Angelique screams, diving for the Beast. He roars and charges Jean when the gun goes off, freezing all of them in place. The Beast looks down uncomprehending at the limp form on the floor next to his paw. She is still, there is no heartbeat in her, and blood is pooling thick and dark across the cold stone.

He is still staring when the curse takes him over. For once, he welcomes it, flees from the horrid sight and retreats, letting Bastien rise to the fore until he's...

... until I am on my hands and knees in Angelique's blood. I touch her neck, searching desperately for a pulse. There isn't one.

"You see," Jean says, "you see how generous I am. She's all yours now."

Shock burns away beneath an explosion of fury in my chest. I hear my own roar and before I have made a conscious decision, I am knocking Lafarge to the ground and my hands are around his throat. He clutches at my wrists in a feeble attempt to dislodge me. He cannot. The Beast gives me his strength, wanting the bastard to die as much as I do. Lafarge's eyes bulge and his tongue sticks out as he turns blue and purple.

I feel hands on me. It takes a lot of them to pry me away from Lafarge and I am fighting them with everything I have to get back and finish the deed. "*It was yours!*" I scream as they drag me away and I know he can still hear me. The entire castle can. "*The child was yours!*"

A blow to the head knocks me out cold.

Chapter Twenty-two

When I wake up, it is still night. I am still human and the castle is dark and silent. I can't hear what's going on downstairs. I'm in my chambers, back in the chains, alone. I bury my face in my hands. I can still see Angelique's dead body in my mind's eye. I am covered in her blood, though it has already dried.

I am shaking but don't understand why. The wind is cold, blowing in from the balcony, but the hearth fire is roaring and my own anger makes me sweat. I want to know what's happening down there. The guards better not have let Lafarge escape. The bastard should be chained in my dungeon, locked away until the Beast wakes. I can feel him now. If he can get his hands on Lafarge, this time he won't hesitate. It should be the Beast who ends Lafarge. He is still merciful enough to make it quick.

Suddenly I sense I am not alone. I look up expecting to see Jacques, a question already on my tongue, but it is a different presence all together.

A hunched figure swathed in a dark, ragged cloak, with one hand smooth and young, the other gnarled and old. She stands in the shadows, as much part of the night as any ghoul risen from the dead.

"You." Can she be a ghost? No. As the clouds shift to uncover the moon, its light falls directly on her. She casts a shadow. She's real enough. "A man can never bury his past, can he?" I say bitterly. "No matter how much he's been made to repay his mistakes." I raise my hands into the light. "In blood."

I would have expected it to be Lilith. If a phantasm from the otherworld is to witness me in this state, it ought to be the one who would derive the most pleasure from my misery. But for all I know, that narcissistic bitch has forgotten all about me. Which begs the question, why hasn't this creature? What is she, anyway?

The hag floats closer like a vision. She glides across the floor as if her feet never touch it and lowers to sit before me. I feel her staring at me for long moments and I say nothing, only stare back. It's strangely satisfying, this wordless communication. I remember it from centuries ago and though it led to all of this, I find I harbor no ill will against her. I even feel something like a smile pull on my lips and I nod to her in belated greeting.

The hag returns the gesture, making me feel as if no time at all has passed since our last meeting.

She produces a deck of tarot cards and places it on the floor between us. The sight of it comforts me. For a moment I forget everything that's happening below stairs and grin outright. "What dark portents do you bring tonight?" I ask. "Haven't you done enough?"

The hag turns a card. The Queen of Cups. As if I need a fucking reminder. Without waiting for my answer, she flips the next one—The Hermit. And the next one—The Moon. The answers I struggled to decipher so long ago, now so glaringly obvious in what I've become. I would laugh at myself if any humor still lingered inside me. Instead, I wait for the next card. If memory serves, it should be Strength. I feel my heart beat faster in anticipation. I need to see her again. Angelique's death robbed me of any strength I possessed.

I've finally found a person more foul than I and was completely powerless against him. I won't do anything as theatrical as letting it destroy me, but for tonight, at least, I cannot think of anything to do besides sit here and brood. If I didn't have hands and feet I'd think I turned into the Beast prematurely. I need my strength back. And right now, the woman I've all but forgotten is the only strength I have left.

Give me a glimpse, I plead silently, feeling that now ancient yearning for her reawaken inside me. *Just a glimpse of her.*

But the card she turns is The Devil, and the hag is pointing at the door. Jean Lafarge. Does she expect me to be surprised?

"What about him?"

She turns the next card—The Hanged Man. And then there is the one I seek. Strength, with its red, red rose and not a hint of the woman I once saw beneath it.

It is reversed.

Dread fills me and I seek the hag's gaze. She raises her head as though to look at me, but I can't see anything of her face. A gnarled hand reaches up and rests on my forehead. A bright flash of light makes me close my eyes and in my mind I see what she is trying to tell me.

I see Lafarge running to the village of Fauve and rousing a mob. I see them marching on the castle and finding Angelique's body, and me in my beastly form. They are not affected by the curse—they can kill the Beast and they will. And once I see myself dead and gone, and my castle weathered inside and out by decades of neglect, my Strength appears, dressed in a pauper's rags, begging for coin on the streets of Fauve. She shivers in the cold and no one will stop to help her, not the baker, or the saw bones, not even the priest.

No one, until Lafarge, an old man already, holds his gloved hand out for her to take.

"*No,*" I gasp out. Not him! That murderous bastard cannot be allowed to touch her! I'd gouge his eyes out before I'd let him even look at her.

I force myself into the vision, bend it to my will and change what I see, make Lafarge go deaf and blind, far away from the woman I feel desperate to protect. But without Lafarge, nothing is different. She's still kneeling in the street, still starving and freezing, and this time, she dies that way, too.

I roar in denial and my hand shoots out blindly to close around the hag's throat. She grasps my wrist with her young hand at that very instant and pries me loose with laughable ease. Her fingers curl into my wrist and the pain is nothing compared to the searing spasm in my chest.

The vision changes and I see Lafarge running from the castle. It's the real him, the present him, not the future. He slows and stops with a frown, looks back at the castle, then at his own empty hands. His face contorts with confusion. He walks the rest of the way slowly and somehow I know his thoughts. He doesn't remember. Not the way it really happened. All he knows is that Angelique cuckolded him with a human man named Bastien Sauvage, and he shot her dead in the man's castle.

The vision goes dark and I fall over, my head spinning. I pass out for the second time that night. When I come to, the hag is gone and so are her cards. All that is left of her is a blood red rose. I clutch the thorny stem, heedless of the pain, as the first light of dawn tears me asunder.

Chapter Twenty-three

The hag's rose is wilting. If it's even hers at all. The flower could have come from anywhere, and the Beast's memories of that night are so distorted he no longer knows what is real and what isn't. It's beyond tempting to simply pretend it was all a bad dream, a figment of Bastien's crazed mind.

But Angelique is real. Was real. Jacques and some of the women moved her body to the ice room and scrubbed the floors of her blood. The Beast can still smell it there, anyway. It is obvious no one will be coming to claim her. The bastard Lafarge probably didn't even tell anyone she is dead. It would be just like him to feign ignorance. All he needs to do is wait long enough for everyone to assume she ran away. After a while, if she doesn't turn up, he'll be able to annul the union and take another wife.

There is only one thing the Beast can do about it.

He has Angelique buried in the garden next to his parents. Though his memory of them is all but nonexistent, he knows they would have welcomed Angelique as their own. The Beast couldn't save the young woman, but perhaps he can give her, in death, the peace she deserved while she was alive.

"You say the hag showed him the woman?" Jacques asks.

"For all I know, it was a hallucination."

"But what if it wasn't?" Jacques says eagerly. "Surely she wouldn't have appeared without reason. It must mean something. She must be close by. If we could just—"

The Beast laughs. "It's been almost three hundred years, Jacques. How much longer will you cling to your hope before you realize it's nothing but an illusion? This is it. This is what our lives will be like for all of eternity."

"There is always a way out of a difficult situation."

"Absolutely," he says. "And it's quite easy. Go and fetch one of the villagers here and watch how quickly he'll find something to skewer me with. Go on, what are you waiting for? Only someone unaffected by the curse can break it, so the solution should be obvious." He shudders as he says the words. His death would break the curse, true, but it would also kill the woman. That surety is there whether he wants to believe it or not. Bastien believes it and that taints the Beast's own perception.

"We don't know what it would do to the rest of us. It might kill us all if you were to die." Apparently, this is something Jacques has considered before.

"Haven't you lived long enough?" The Beast sounds weary saying it.

"I have existed far too long," Jacques agrees. "But it is a state not to be confused with living. None of us have been living these three centuries. We haven't changed, aged, grown up, had children, or died. That, Master, is not life. And, while I would be most content to... cease, I would not presume to make that choice for the others. Would you?"

He leaves before the Beast can think of anything to say.

The library is in the middle of repairs, all the books neatly packed out of harm's way. With nothing to do, the Beast strolls aimlessly through his castle. He knows each stone, each tapestry and every painting by heart. While the west wing where he resides is bursting with life, the east wing is dusty and abandoned; there is no one to use these rooms anymore. The Beast himself hardly ever has reason to venture here.

Some faint fragment of a memory takes him to one of the south-facing rooms. The door is stuck from disuse and everything inside is covered with white sheets. A balcony, easily twice as large as his own, opens off the south wall. Glass doors let in all the best light and frame a magnificent view of the forests and mountains.

This used to be Bastien's studio. In the absence of his parents to oversee his education, Jacques hired tutors and prescribed a wide range of subjects for the young prince to study. Art used to be one of his favorites.

The Beast tugs on a white sheet and it slides off an easel. Another reveals a table laden with dried, cracked paints. In the corner is a stack of canvases, darkened with age, but still usable. The Beast mounts one on the easel. His paw is too big to hold a delicate brush, but he can just manage to grasp a piece of coal.

He draws a curve, then another, and another, until a shape begins to appear. It's rough, clumsy. He knows he can do better. Setting the canvas aside, he takes another and starts over. A face appears, the curve of one shoulder, but the features elude him.

Another canvas replaces that one. He takes his time, conjures his subject in his thoughts as vividly as he can before he traces what he sees in his mind's eye onto the canvas. Yes, that's it. The blank space fills with an outline, then shading. It's imperfect. Black and gray could never hope to capture what he is trying to draw.

Frustrated, he reaches for the final canvas. There won't be any more chances unless he sends his driver to the fairs. Eyeing the dried paints and rotted bushes, the Beast drops the piece of coal and bounds out of the east wing, shouting for Jacques. "Canvas," he tells the startled butler. "As much of it as you can find. And paints and brushes, the best money can buy. Quickly! Before the merchants leave."

He waits around only long enough to make certain his orders are being followed and then returns to the studio and the coal.

It's harder now, he is unsure of his dexterity. Only the lightest of strokes will do, and his heavy paw almost crushes the coal to dust in an effort to keep the lines as delicate as possible. His concentration is so absolute he almost doesn't notice when Bastien rouses within him. His human side can see the subject on the square of canvas as easily as the Beast.

Bastien moves the Beast's hand over the surface, slowly tracing her eyes and nose. The waves of her hair cascade in a graceful fall around her face, caressing the line of her throat. The mouth takes them the longest. It's soft when the coal would have it appear hard. The lower lip is fuller than the upper, lush and enticing. She is smiling just a little, with just a hint of a secret tucked into the corners of her mouth as she looks over her bare shoulder at something to Beast's left.

It's her...

Chapter Twenty-four

The moment I awaken I root beneath my pillow for the hidden key. Sweet little Jocelyn. She hid it so well not even the Beast could find it. I've been saving this for something special. Something well worth the punishment it will incur when I unlock these shackles.

The chains that bind me fall away and I am free for the first time in centuries. There is a pair of pants set out on the chair. I dress with haste and exit my chambers. The guards shout a warning, but I ignore them and run straight to the east wing. It's still my goddamned castle and I can go wherever the hell I please.

They give chase and rouse half the damn staff with their yelling for no good reason. I let them catch me at the studio door. They are winded and out of sorts, easy to defeat, if I should decide to do so. I don't, and after a few minutes of the three of us just standing there while a crowd of gawkers gathers, I shake them loose. "Stay outside," I growl, thoroughly annoyed at how long it takes them to collect their jaws off the floor and release me. I close the door in their stunned faces.

The Beast has been busy in my absence. The studio is a mess of splattered paints and canvases ruined by his heavy paw. He's kept all of them, carefully stacked all around like the makings of some holy shrine to his talent—or lack thereof. I root around in the stacks for the one I want. There are three relatively salvageable scrawls among these. In one, she is seated regal as a queen on the settee in the library. In another, she is standing in the garden, her eyes closed as she smells a rose bloom. In the third, she is asleep in my bed, her hair spread out on my pillow, her hand slightly curled by her face.

I want none of them. These are the Beast's fantasies, not mine.

The one I seek is just by the door, half hidden by a drawing of a rag doll and a canvas accidentally punched out of its frame. I pull it out carefully and set it on the easel. It took more concentration than I thought possible to make the Beast set this one aside before he ruined it.

This is her, my Strength, the way she ought to look always. The Beast traced her hair adequately, the long waves flowing over her back, baring one shoulder. I trace the line of her lips with my fingertips, brush the rise of her cheek, her temple. She is perfect. Sensual and innocent, strong yet delicate.

I stare at her for a long time, not trusting myself to pick up a paint brush and ruin the near divinity of her face. Eventually I realize the night is passing me by and soon the Beast will rise again to take her away from me. I could hate him just for that. His drawings are stick figures compared to the masterpiece I intend to finish. I can see her coming alive for me and my hand reaches for a brush.

I paint with measured haste, conscious of the time and what little I have left, as well as the delicacy of the task before me. A single careless stroke could ruin her. Very soon her skin begins to take on the tone of warmth and seduction. I paint her lips a teasing pink, and her eyes the purest blue I can emulate.

There's not enough time. All too soon the sun is rising and I've just enough time to hide her out of harm's way before I disappear.

The Beast is too busy butchering his own sketches to notice the time and I awake directly in the studio. My pants are in shreds, but I don't care, just as he didn't when he tore them. I set my Beauty on the easel at once. Her hair is tricky. It takes careful alchemy to mix just the right amount of each shade to create the rich hue of auburn and even when I think I have achieved it, the minutest of faults make me return to her again and again to get everything just... perfect.

The servants stop bothering to restrain me. Since both the Beast and I spend most of our time in the studio we are rarely in my chambers to be chained. But as long as I don't stray outside of it, the guards don't seem to care what I do. It suits my purposes.

For years this goes on, the Beast drawing his scenes as I paint my Strength three nights at a time and hide the progress where I know he will never look if he has something of his own to focus on. My obsession is absolute. Perhaps it's why I never feel him rise inside me to look at her through my eyes; why he doesn't seem to remember my mind when I'm gone, nor I his when I wake. We don't want to. We have her now and neither of us is willing to share.

Little by little, my Strength comes to life beneath my brush. Her long lashes cast a soft shadow against her cheek, minuscule flecks of green light up her eyes, her face glows with some inner light I know I will never feel, and her lips glisten enticingly, until all I can think of is kissing them.

She is naked in my vision, but positioned in such a way that only her bare shoulder hints at her nudity—turned sideways, her arms crossed to cover her breasts, one delicate hand resting against her shoulder. The curvature of her silhouette is only hinted at with a play of shadow and shading, and the canvas cuts her off at the hip. It is just large enough to make her appear lifelike, as if she could step out of the portrait at any moment.

But she is not finished.

In the fifth year since I beheld her outline, I add the final detail, one that, thinking back, never should have marred her effortless grace. I cannot help myself. My hand moves of its own accord, tracing the outline of an object that ought to be alien to her. Somehow, it is not. It's as much part of her as it is of me—the symbol of my curse and my redemption alike.

Petal after petal, a blood red rose appears in her hand. The bloom is so large that even resting against her shoulder it just brushes the line of her jaw. A foreign, heavy layer of paint added to an already magnificent work of art and still the cursed thing seem so natural I don't know why it wasn't there from the beginning.

On the third and final night of another full moon, I am finished. The brush drops from my numb fingers as I step back to behold the most beautiful creature I have ever dared to dream. I reach out a hand, half expecting her skin to warm to my touch. My torment is complete.

And I realize I will never see her.

If she did not appear in the three hundred years of my imprisonment, she never will. And even if she somehow does, as the hag foretold, the Beast will never let her near me. The selfish bastard will keep her all to himself to shield her from my wicked ways. He will chain me again, high up in that goddamned tower, far away where no one will hear my cries. She will never even know I exist, and with the Beast playing the gentleman, the tormented victim, she will never even wonder at his other side.

In that moment, I despise the Beast with every fiber of my cursed being.

But he is part of me and there is only so much hate I can stomach before it turns outward and then I hate her. That teasing little smile, the mischievous glint in her eyes, the way she is completely bare, yet I still can't see more than the merest hint of her flesh.

I hurl the palette against the wall and pick up a knife just as the sun is about to rise. I manage to cut a long, satisfyingly jagged line across the canvas before the bastard takes me over.

The Beast awakens to a knife in his paw, lying on the floor of the studio. He groans in residual pain and confusion as he throws the blade away and rises. His claws scratch into paint and he immediately raises that paw off a finished portrait.

Breath leaves him at the sight. It's her, far more lifelike than his clumsy drawings could ever make her, and she is magnificent. Stunning.

And Bastien has wrecked her.

His heart breaks at the cut that rips across her face. What sort of monster would do such a thing, destroy something so beautiful?

Bastien would.

The Beast gently picks up the painting. He will not set it on the easel; won't leave it in this dusty place. He carries his Beauty back to his chambers and hangs her portrait on the wall facing the window. A place of honor, where he can look upon her each morning.

It is there, gazing into her bright blue eyes, that he realizes that if, by some miracle of mercy, she is real and finds her way to the Beast, he can never trust her safety to Bastien.

He will never risk her around his human half.

If she is real, he vows, she will never know the monster in a human skin exists.

Chapter Twenty-five

My prison becomes inescapable. The Beast, having caught on to my subtle subconscious manipulations, shuts me out of his thoughts so thoroughly I can't even see or hear what he does. But it takes effort and wearies him, and when he sleeps, I make certain to exact my revenge, invading his dreams and twisting them my way—any way, really, as long as he doesn't enjoy them.

When I am awake each month, my chains are unbreakable and the key is gone. The bastard even locks balcony door and all windows so I can't smell the night air. On the nights it rains, my rage at this knows no bounds. I can almost scent the rain in my chambers, but never quite enough. My lungs burn with the need to inhale that fresh, cold wind. I am denied.

I lash out again and again at anything I can get my hands on, more of a wild animal than the Beast ever allows himself to be. Only once do I reach for the painting. The Beast set it where it might best mock me from its high perch on the wall. It's not quite high enough. I tear it down and rip into it until it's in strips and tatters.

The Beast's agonized wail when he discovers it the next morning crushes me. He doesn't want me to, but I feel what he feels—utter, terrible loss. And I realize I just destroyed the only solace I will ever have, the only likeness of her I will ever behold with my own eyes.

That is why, when the sun goes down again, I try to pick up where the Beast left off; try to salvage what I can. His clumsiness in gluing pieces of canvas onto the backing all but ensures it will never be whole again. Whatever I can do is too little too late.

With a heavy heart, I hang the ruined portrait back in its place of honor and do not go near it again. I become my own jailer, silently seething night and day. I fight my own quiet battle, let the Beast think he got the best of me.

He'll never be rid of me. I am Lord Bastien Sauvage III, Duke of Colline, forgotten cousin to a long dead king. I am a prince of this kingdom, and the true master of this castle.

I wear the curse of the Beast, not him, and no matter how hard he tries to keep me from the world, he cannot keep me from his memories of it. I know how he broods day and night, closed away in his library, with all his precious books. I see the way the servants look upon him, with less pity and more impatience every day. I feel the seasons change, the rain in his fur and the snow beneath his paws.

And I feel when things begin to change. I feel the wicked Faery wind behind the gathering clouds, the sting of Lilith's spell in its lightning and frigid rain. I sense the lost merchant stumble into my home.

That this pathetic looking human would be the first in over three centuries to brave trespassing on my lands is baffling, yet I know it was desperation which drove him to it—there is nowhere else for him to take shelter from the wretched storm. He has nothing but the clothes on his back, drenched through and half frozen as they are, and a near empty wagon pulled by an aging, limping pony.

His fear is sickening. The way the servants pander to his favor as if he is an honored guest they fear will depart too soon makes me glad I am not in possession of my body to wring all their necks. The Beast finds it more than irksome, too. He growls when the hostlers take charge of the pony, snarls when the cook stokes the fire for a midnight meal for the "poor lost soul," and terrifies the merchant nearly to death when he roars from the shadows to see Aimee show him to a guest room.

But he never shows his monstrous face.

Through the Beast's glowing eyes I watch the merchant shiver during the relentless storm and sleep fitfully through the night to awake the next morning. More is the pity. I see him wander into the garden as if it belongs to him and cut a single blood red rose. It is the one the Beast holds closest to his heart, for it looks like the rose in the portrait.

I amuse myself by spurring my jailer forward. I would happily see the merchant torn to ragged shreds, but the Beast pulls back before his claws cut more than the dirty linen of the merchant's shirt.

More terror saturates the air we breathe until even I am sick with it.

"Please," the man cries. "I meant no harm! I-I lost my way in the storm. Have mercy, my Lord Beast."

I laugh as the Beast roars furiously. "You dare mock me, human!"

"No, please! Please, I beg you…"

"This is how you repay your host's generosity? I spared your life in the night, gave you shelter through the storm, and this is my thanks! I should toss you in the dungeon!"

The merchant is shaking so much it takes him three tries to turn to his belly and prostrate himself before the Beast. "I beg forgiveness. I only… it's for my daughter. Please, let me pay you for the rose. I meant no offense, only a gift for my daughter…"

The man's heartfelt pleas don't move either of us. It's the way he desperately, foolishly, starts on a litany about his offspring's charms that makes us both quiet. He describes a great, selfless beauty, a strong, brave heart, and a quick mind. The youngest of three, a girl with a kind soul forever seeking goodness between the pages of books. A father's pride, nothing more.

Yet something in that eulogy—for that is what it is—stirs a memory inside me. I see myself painting a red rose onto soft skin and that luscious mouth smiling at me in a gentle tease. I see a dream from so long ago it hardly seems real. A painted world, a wolf howling at the moon, and a woman standing before me. Her eyes are brave, but pleading at the same time. I couldn't hear her that first time. I hear her now. "Find me," she says. "Please, Bastien, help me!"

After all these years I know better than to overlook a portent as powerful as this. If there's the smallest chance the hag's vision was true, I will not ignore it.

I whisper in my jailer's ear the merest hint of an idea.

"This girl," the Beast says curiously, "you love her very much."

"Yes, my... Monsieur. With all my heart. More than my own life."

And there it is. The Beast narrows his eyes. "Let's see if this saint of yours is capable of the same. I will release you unharmed and give you my best horse to take you home."

The merchant looks up with wide eyes filled with hope. "Oh, thank you! Thank you!"

The Beast picks up the felled rose between his claws and holds it out to the man. "You will deliver your gift to your daughter and send her here to take your place."

The man's face becomes white as a ghost and for long moments he cannot speak. "No," he finally pleads. "Kill me if you must, but spare my daughter."

The Beast roars. "*You dare defy me!*"

There are tears in the merchant's eyes. His heart beats too fast. I can almost feel it breaking. I have no sympathy for his plight, and neither does the Beast. "I... can't," the human whispers brokenly.

"But you will," the Beast assures him without mercy. "I will see the youngest of your daughters in my castle in two day's time, or I will come for her myself and take her from you, along with everything else you hold dear."

The merchant drops his face into his hands and weeps.

An odd swirl of triumph and disappointment overtake the Beast, and me along with him. The servants are spying from inside the castle, their disapproving regard a heavy weight on the Beast. "You fear she will not do this." It is an accusation.

"To save me, I fear she will. I fear she will pay a high price for her selflessness. And her father's folly. Please, Monsieur, I would ask again. Take my life and spare her."

The Beast growls.

"But you will not," the merchant says, a man who's lost all hope with one slice of a knife through the stem of a precious rose. Head bent in supplication, he says, "Then I can only beg for you to have mercy on my Lyssette."

The simple entreaty, spoken purely out of love, humbles the Beast. "You have my word she will come to no harm at my hands." That he says it to me as much as the merchant galls me.

I am powerless to stop the man from leaving once the decree is passed.

The Beast is half crazed with anticipation, waiting for the merchant to make good on his word, else risk his terrible wrath. He has the gravel beneath his paws three times, impatient to do something, schooling himself not to. Pacing before the hearth, ears trained for any hint of a sound that might announce an approaching rider.

When she walks through the door, not even the strongest of restraints can keep me from looking out from deep within the Beast to behold her face. The truth of her stuns me. I mocked a father's pride, never thinking he might be understating his child's virtues. She is just as I painted her, only so much more. She is sunshine and tempest, grace and integrity. She's a magnificent summer storm and the gentlest, wide eyed doe. She makes the Beast maudlin with metaphors until I silence his mind and call her just one.

Not Strength.

Hope.

I watch through his eyes as she calls him names. I listen with his ears to her soft footsteps as she explores the castle. I feel his joy when she finds the library, and I hear his thoughts as he plans for the next full moon.

With Mademoiselle Lyssette, my torment and my savior at last inside my castle, I stay quiet and do nothing. The hag painted my future with her cards. She showed me my salvation, and after more than three hundred years, here she is. No matter what the Beast does, she is my destiny, not his. He can try to keep me from her, but he will never be able to keep her from finding me.

That certainty gives me the satisfaction I need to patiently while away the first full moon.

I bide my time and wait.

The End

The Beast

Chapter One

Don't go past the anteroom, he warned me, claws worrying his tattered shirt. *You cannot trust anything that comes out of his mouth. Promise me, Lyssette, promise you'll remember it's not me.*

I promised.

I remember my vow as I lay a shaky hand on the door's handle. The guard is in the nook, in place of one of the armors. He nods to me in encouragement, but I know he is wary. He knows what is inside that room, and, like his master, he does not want me to see it.

But I must.

I worry, but not enough to turn back. I have seen this man, my Beast, in the midst of a rage, terrible fangs flashing as he roared to the skies. I have seen his vicious strength as he brought down wild animals in defense of me. I can look upon his monstrous visage now and see the gentle soul that dwells inside.

If I can do that, I need to do this, too.

I wish you would reconsider.

I didn't. I cannot.

I have already accepted everything else about my Beast. Though his claws frightened me at first, they have never harmed me, nor have his fangs. Though he is giant in height and strength, he takes such care when he moves that I no longer worry walking beside him. I have come to love everything he thought would scare me away.

Why should this be any different?

"My lady," the guard says and I realize I haven't moved.

"I am all right," I tell him. He is here to keep me safe, and I can see by the look in his eyes that he is prepared to do his duty. He has orders to put my life above his master's and, though it will pain him, he will do what he must if it should come to that.

It worries me far more than the monster waiting beyond this closed door.

I do not let it show.

The handle is rusty and sticks as I unlatch the door. It is heavy, but I manage to push it open enough to pass through. I should close it behind me, I know, but cannot seem to bring myself to do it; the anteroom is fully dark and I crave the light of the hallway to guide me.

I hear breathing farther in the chamber, by the window. My heart throbs and I am unsteady in the pitch black room. I pick my way carefully, move slowly, allowing my eyes to adjust to the darkness.

I can see faint shadows of forms now. The windows I walk toward are giant, but covered with drapes. Even so I can make out the full moon's glow.

A rustle of movement makes me hesitate.

Chains rattle, and I know. I know he senses me near. My palms are moist. I clutch my skirts tight and make myself move forward.

A sharp inhale. "Ah," he breathes. "Company." I scarcely recognize the voice.

The chains tumble to the floor and I hear him moving, dragging them behind, to one side of the room. The spark he makes to light a candle cracks like lightning in the room and makes me flinch. One candle lights another, and another, and still another, until the entire room is aglow. I am at the edge of the anteroom now. This is as far as I am to go.

His back is to me, a ragged shirt hanging on a frame that looks deceptively sparse in it. But where the neck gapes to his shoulder I can see muscle. The massive manacles encircling his wrists and ankles were each too heavy for me to lift when my Beast showed them to me yesterday. But this creature is not hindered by them in the least. Indeed, he adjusts them as I would a delicate bracelet.

My mouth is dry, I am far more nervous than I expected to be.

He stoops to the fireplace, flicks his arm sideways to move the heavy chains out of his way so he can light a fire. "So you finally got the courage," he says.

"Y-you know who I am?"

He chuckles, more of a scoff. "Oh, I know." He turns and I see his profile, backlit by the fire. He has long wooden stick in his hand to tend the fire; there are no iron pokers in this room. Nothing he could use to free himself. "You think I don't hear your sniveling voice every month? You think I don't smell that disgusting sewer water you call perfume all over my home?" He shoves to his feet and I flinch.

Worse, he notices. Though I cannot see his face clearly, I … sense his amusement.

"I hear the servants talk about you like some goddamned salvation. They all think you're a saint come to do battle with the Devil himself. Well?" He snaps the chains like a silken train and comes around the massive bed, into the light. "What do you think of him?"

Dark golden strands of hair fall over the face of a fallen angel. Strong jaw, proud nose, dark brows and a hard, twisted mouth. But his eyes… They aren't what I expected to see. They are empty. Cold. Eyes of a true monster.

Promise me.

I promised. And I can see it now. This is not my Beast.

He sneers. "You're no savior. I know exactly what you are. You're the bitch who thinks to banish me. From my own house, no less. Harridan," he accuses, his fury rising with each word. My Beast could never be so cruel. "Trespasser. Interloper. *Whore!*" No, this is not my Beast.

But this *was* my Beast.

Before he became cursed.

Chapter Two

I ran. His roar followed me all the way to the opposite wing. I could still hear him when I locked myself in my room. Or perhaps I merely imagined that.

Now, in the harsh light of day, I stand before a mirror and behold a coward. My gown is blue today, to bring out my eyes, but all I see is the dark tinge beneath them and the sallow paleness of my skin. Sylvie did all she could to make my auburn curls shine, but none of it can hide the truth.

No matter how many times I pinch my cheeks, I cannot bring colour into them. My lips feel dry as dust. I am weary, and ashamed.

My Beast is no doubt waiting for me, but I cannot bear to face him.

Oh, Lyssette, why are you here?

I make myself walk down the grand staircase, past the whispering servants with their pitying gazes, into the small solarium where I usually break fast with my host. Today, it is empty.

"Lady Lyssette."

I face Jacques, about to tell him yet again not to address me as a lady, but the look on his face stops me. "Where is he?" I ask.

"The master bid me to send his apologies," Jacques says. "He regrets he will not be able to perform his duty as host today."

"His duty?" The word chills me.

I can see in Jacques' eyes something is terribly amiss. "I believe," he says, "the master feels rather the worse for wear after…"

Does he remember? Does he have any recollection at all of our meeting last night? "I understand," I say. "Can you tell me where he is?"

"I'm afraid he does not wish to be disturbed. The master has instructed me to provide you with anything you wish. He has even made his carriage available to you, if that is what you desire."

"Did he?" I feel my ire return some pink into my cheeks. The anger is a welcome spark of fire to the cold weight in my gut. "Does he expect me to leave? Is this some sort of fare well?"

Jacques looks away. In all my time here, I have never known him to do such a thing.

"H-has he given up, then?"

The loyal butler swings his head to look at me once more, his eyes wide. He smoothes his expression expertly, but his voice is unsteady when he speaks. "Please understand, my lady. The master has come a ways since his curse. We all see it, though he cannot." There is deep emotion in his words. He is telling me something he ought not.

I listen.

"But with every rise of the full moon, he is transformed, reminded of what he used to be. He is not allowed to forget. It is part of his punishment to remember his sins, and it has become much more of a burden than…"

So he remembers. I tell Jacques, as bravely as I can, "Please inform your master that his guest is determined to stay. And that I shall see him again tonight."

Jacques draws himself up, I see relief and joy in him, but though I notice his mouth quirk in a suppressed smile, he says, "Apologies, my lady, but the master has forbidden you to enter his chambers again. He fears it is not safe for you to do so at this time."

"Because the moon peaks full tonight?"

Jasques inclines his head. "It has proven to be the most ... trying in the past."

"I see." I smooth my skirts. I need that moment to collect my thoughts. "Then please tell him he has nothing to fear. I shall amuse myself reading this evening."

"I shall inform the master." He bows and leaves quietly.

I eat by myself, watching the gardeners tend the blooms outside the window. When I finish, I convey my thanks to the cook and remove myself to the library. It is stunning, filled with books large and small, stories of adventure and love, volumes on every subject known to man. I could spend eternity familiarizing myself with those printed words, though, on this day, I do not allow myself the luxury of exploration. As I have told Jacques, I will be reading tonight.

But I will not be alone.

I choose my book with care.

Chapter Three

Tonight I do not hesitate. I know what awaits me now. I smile at the guard. Louis seems nervous but he squares his shoulders and nods to me. Book in hand, I enter the beast's lair.

Tonight there is light aplenty to see by. I see the torn rags, the shattered chairs. I see part of the table in the blazing fireplace. I do not let my reaction show.

The man who is my Beast is pacing, nearly snarling. He truly is like a restrained wild thing, snapping his chains, futilely fighting for his freedom. With all his strength and fury he cannot break free. I take heart in that.

"You again," he snarls, baring his teeth.

I gather my courage and smile. "I have come to sit with you a while."

The man rushes toward me, but the chains pull him up short. His fingers curl into claws, as though he wants to tear into me. His massive chest rises and falls; his entire body shudders, strains. He is livid. "Get out," he hisses.

I take a step toward him, but not too close. "You do not frighten me," I say in the face of his wrath.

Malice burns cold in his blue eyes. "You think you can pull the tiger's tail while he is chained? I won't be chained forever. You *should* fear me, little girl. When I am free, I will show you no mercy."

"I am sure," I tell him, pretending that it was the cold draft sending chills down my spine and not his words. "But until then, you are here, and I am not leaving."

He grinds his teeth so much I can hear it. I've no doubt that if he was free, he would make good on his threats and tear me limb from limb.

But he is not free, and that makes me brave. Perhaps even a little reckless. My smile is more confident this time. "Now, will you be a gentleman and offer me a seat, or do I need to look for one myself?"

What he says next does not bear repeating. I swallow a shocked gasp and turn my burning cheeks away as I search for a chair. There isn't one. I can discern bits and pieces, but not one survived his wrath.

He sneers. His chains drop loudly to the floor as he reaches down, never taking his eyes off me. The chair leg he grasps is still loosely attached to the rest of its body. The chained wild thing stomps on it viciously to sever the connection.

He looks at it, then at me, as though weighing his options. Clearly dissatisfied, he hurls the broken piece of wood onto the voracious flame.

Undaunted, I gather some cushions and make a nest of sorts where the light is bright enough to read by and settle in. "Now then—" I scream as a vase shatters a mere hand width from me. Shards explode all around me, I can feel them rain onto my hair.

"Get out!" he roars.

Louis rushes in, sword drawn, taking a stand between me and the crazed master of this castle.

The chained beast laughs, a sound full of hatred. The guard is no more a threat to him than I am, and he knows it.

"My lady, are you hurt?"

"My lady," my host mimics cruelly. "Get her out of my sight," he orders. "She is not to step foot in here again." He turns to address me directly. "I may not be able to get rid of you, but I fucking well don't have to look at you while you're here."

My heart is racing, but I will it to calm. "I am all right, thank you Louis."

"Perhaps you should—"

"I am not going anywhere," I tell him, hardly wincing at my sharp tone. "I have a book to read."

"I ordered you to remove her!"

Louis lowers his sword, incensing his master beyond reason. "Then may I suggest moving out of the line of fire, my lady?"

I want to argue, but my ungracious host is already reaching for another weapon. "Yes, that is a wonderful idea."

Louis calls for a mirror, so that I may still see the beast from around the corner. The monster breaks it immediately, but it remains in place. When everything is ready, Louis leaves and I settle in once more.

"Now then," I say. "The Little Red Riding Hood…"

I sit until my legs go numb. I read until my voice is hoarse. Through the bluster, the curses and threats, through the constant onslaught of anything and everything he can throw, I read to him.

He screams. Vows to kill me, tear me apart with his bare hands, and things far worse. I believe him. If not for the chains, I know he would cause me every pain a man can possibly inflict on a woman. This is the true beast of the castle.

And for the first time, I truly believe he deserved his curse. I want the monster to suffer, because I know that everything he threatens, he has done before. This… thing, the demon wearing a human mask is so different from the creature I have come to know and love that I can hardly believe they are one and the same.

Tears blur the words on the page. *What am I to do?*

I can think of nothing else, but to persevere. I cannot fight him on his terms. And so I must be patient and wait him out, somehow coax him to fight by my rules. For now, I have my book.

He has no more things to throw, but I can still hear him raging. I glance up and see dozens of his reflections in the broken mirror. He is tearing his bed apart, linens, mattress, everything to get to the wooden frame.

I duck my head and read on.

The frame shatters. I brace for another wave of attack.

It doesn't come.

I hear him groan; look up to see him doubled over, clutching his head.

He screams in terrible pain and, before my very eyes, he begins to change.

I lose my breath, the book forgotten. The clock face is broken, it no longer ticks to tell the time. But I can see faint light vaguely outline the draperies.

Dawn.

The transformation is gruesome and brings me to my feet. My legs nearly buckle, but I stumble to the doorway, terrified for the man-beast in the destroyed room.

He screams and roars, shaking with pain, and grief, and such horrible shame. My heart bleeds, weeping for him. I fall to my knees, helpless to do anything but watch.

When it is finally, blessedly over, my Beast bows his head, looking utterly exhausted. His rumbling breaths are a comfort like nothing I've ever known.

I cannot give up on the monster of a man. For this gentle, tormented Beast, I must fight on. I must find a way to free him.

"I'm here," I sob.

He stops breathing. His massive head raises, and blue eyes meet mine. He looks stunned, disbelieving.

I smile, try to offer what little comfort I can.

My Beast makes a sound like a mortally wounded animal. His leonine face drops into his claws and he turns away from me. "Leave me," he says.

Utter, soul shattering defeat makes me obey.

Chapter Four

I stand before the gates of Hell for the third time. I cannot say what brings me here tonight. By all rights, I should be fleeing this place, never to look back. Last night inspired a new flare of despair among the castle's residents. They look at me now, and I know they wonder the same thing I do.

Why is she still here?

Why do this?

Could it work?

They fear me now, and despise me. I give them reason to hope. So long as their master suffers his curse, they, too, are bound to this place. Never to leave, never to change, until he does. The curse is eternal. There is not one man, woman, or child in this place who will tell me how long it has already lasted. And if I build up their hopes for release and fail…

I should leave. Standing here before the closed portal, I want to leave.

The door seems far heavier than it did the night before last when I finally push it open.

Someone—Jacques, I believe—ordered the chambers to be cleaned. There is nothing in the anteroom, aside from lit wall sconces and that broken mirror. It is covered now. I push the tattered velvet aside to expose the cracked surface. I have not yet dared to look into the main chamber. I want the reflection to lessen the impact of its appearance, but it does not.

The monster's bedroom is empty as well. Save for a pallet on the floor and wood enough to last the night, there is nothing. It resembles a cave; a wounded animal's den.

To my shock, he looks wounded. Curled on the pallet on the floor, swaddled in a torn blanket, he shivers. It seems he has not yet realized I am here. He looks so much like my Beast did this morning after the transformation, I feel compelled to go to him. I stop my feet from crossing the threshold. This might be precisely what he is waiting for.

"Are you ill?" I ask.

The man on the floor, looking utterly pathetic, opens one eye, just barely. He moans. "You again." His voice seems weak. What is this? Some sort of elaborate trick? "Haven't I run you out yet?" A massive shudder passes through him.

"What is the matter with you? Should I call for help?"

"Mind your own fucking business," he snarls, but though his voice is cold as ice, I can see the effort it takes him to utter the words.

I trace my steps back to the door. Louis is standing guard in the hallway again. I ask him to have a chaise brought to the anteroom. Within moments, two footmen come bearing the heavy piece of furniture. The monster watches this with seething hatred, but does not utter a sound until they leave.

"Why are you still here?"

It is the same question I see in every face and every set of eyes in this castle. "Because I love the Beast, and so I must learn to love you, too. You and he are one and the same."

He scoffs and it turns into a cough. "Is that what he told you?"

"That is not necessary. I've seen it with my own eyes."

"Horse shit," he says. "You cannot possibly understand, unless you feel it on your own skin."

I am becoming inured to his profanities. "Enlighten me, then."

That one eye opens again, mocking me. "Come closer," he says.

"No."

He chuckles and his body shudders again. When he speaks, his teeth are clenched and his voice strained, as though he has no control over his movements. "There is another way to break the curse. I'd bet this castle he hasn't told you that."

He is toying with me. I know this, and yet I still strain forward to hear more. "How?"

"By the simple fact that he and I are *not* one and the same." He pulls the blanket closer around him, curling more in on himself. "Only one can exist at any one time and that moping bastard somehow managed to get the full month, while I have to make do with three days of it. We are each other's obstacle. Get rid of the obstacle and the possibilities are endless."

"Get rid of... you mean kill? *Kill* one of you?"

"Why do you think they chain me? It can't be done by someone affected by the curse. But accidents do happen."

"You would kill yourself?"

His laugh is pure evil. "Stupid bitch. Why would I do that?"

I feel cold and put my feet up on the chaise like a little child frightened of the dark.

He sees. The monster struggles to sit up, mirroring my pose, but even in his condition he makes it look much more threatening than weak. His eyes reflect the fire's golden glow, making them look almost green. "So tell me, *Savior*," he says the word as an insult. "Would you kill me to forever free the beast? Or would you free the man to reclaim his home and his life?"

Chapter Five

I do not see my Beast the next day. Or the day after, or the day after that. Not a glimpse, not one word. It is as though he is not in the castle any longer. Life goes on as it always has: The maids clean, the chefs cook, the gardeners tend the blooms and orchards. I am presented with magnificent feasts at each meal, but I eat them alone. I stroll the beautiful grounds around this majestic structure, but my step is heavy with loneliness.

I have much on my mind, and I imagine my Beast does as well.

But I hear the servants whispering. They will not speak to me directly, no doubt for fear of their master. Nevertheless, on the sixth day, I learn the reason for the monster's weakened condition on that final, awful night, as well as the absence of my host now.

On my way to the library, resigned to yet another day without my Beast, I come upon two maids in the dining room. Their voices carry through the door and I quietly ease to it to better hear Jocelyn speaking to her aunt Aimee.

"Why would he do it?" the girl on the verge of becoming a woman asks. "He could have died!"

"The master is too clever for that," Aimee replies, but I can hear uncertainty in her voice.

"He must have known the lady Lyssette could handle herself with him. She's done it before. She's seen him at his worst!"

"Child, it is not so simple a thing," Aimee says patiently.

I cautiously peek through the key hole.

"Do not call me that," Jocelyn says and stomps her foot. "I am not a child anymore. I haven't been for a long time."

Aimee's hands pause while smoothing the linens they are folding. She looks as though Jocelyn's words hurt her. "I know," she says. "But there are things you can only understand when you fall in love. It is not the lady Lyssette the master doesn't trust. It is himself. It is because she's seen him at his worst that he wanted to protect her from it."

"And so he poisoned himself to keep her safe?"

I gasp, and my hand flies to my mouth to muffle the sound. My heart races and I feel faint. *Poison?* The word... the idea that he would do such a thing for my sake makes me ill. No, it cannot be true. Surely, Jocelyn is mistaken.

"Leave be, Jocelyn," Aimee says. She does not correct the girl. She does not offer another explanation.

I seek the wall for support as my legs go weak. It is true, then. He poisoned himself to keep the monster docile. Did he... could he have known that his words are as much a weapon as his powerful arms?

"But he could have died!" Jocelyn insists with so much feeling, it sounds as though she is on the verge of tears. She sounds the way I feel. Frantic, hurt, astonished that the Beast would do such a thing. She sounds as if she would race to his chambers at once to berate him for his recklessness, or perhaps to nurse him back to health.

Aimee hears the same thing I do. "Jocelyn!" she hisses sternly. "You must stop this wretched infatuation. You know you cannot break the curse for him. Remember your place, girl! You're a maid in the master's household. Nothing more."

I wonder how long the girl has loved her master. Since the beginning? Did she love him before he became cursed? Did he make her believe he could love her back? *Would* he have loved her back, if I hadn't come along?

Jocelyn was always kind to me, as all the others were. She would be my chamber maid, had I not insisted that I do not need one. She is a beautiful girl, with black hair and eyes the clearest green, like jewels. Any man would be lucky to have her. Many young men here gaze at her with longing, but she has eyes for none.

None, apparently, except her master.

I feel pity for her. It is no easy thing to love the Beast. How much more difficult must it be to love him, and know he will never love her back?

I remove myself from the hallway; let my feet carry me wherever they will. My mind is in a daze, swirling with so many questions I know I might never get answers to. I think about every person here, and how long they must have waited for even a chance to break the spell. How many of them hated their master for being the cause of their misery? How many wished, even once, that he would die?

How many have loved him always, despite his flaws, choosing to see only the good in him, even when they had to imagine it to be there?

I find myself in front of his chambers. There are no guards on duty today and the hallway is dark and quiet. I enter without knocking. As I expected, it is empty. I walk across the anteroom, and for the first time enter the monster's bedroom. The chains lie in a heap in one corner. I hesitate to touch them. They're stained with blood from his struggles to free himself.

The fireplace is cold, a mound of ash and soot the only evidence of life. I pull the heavy drapes aside to reveal magnificent windows and a glass door leading out to a balcony. It overlooks the courtyard. From here, I can see the abandoned road for miles beyond the dark forest. I see my village in the distance. I think of my father, and my sisters. It has been months since I have seen them last. I pray they are well.

As I turn away, my gaze snares on a portrait hanging on the wall. It is ruined, torn to pieces, many of them missing. What remains of the canvas hangs in strips along the sides, twisted to hide their subject.

I have seen similar paintings around the castle, set aside to be disposed of. Portraits of my Beast, and the man he used to be, each torn as though one part of him could not stand to look at the other.

I can imagine him stalking through the castle, seeking them out to tear them apart. As man, and as beast, each refusing to abide any hint of the other's existence.

This one is different, I know. It has not been put away. It hangs in its proper place, a place of honor in the middle of the wall, where sunlight from the windows shines directly upon it. Why keep this one? What significance does it have?

Curiosity compels me closer. If I move the pieces back together, will I see the Beast, or the man?

With careful fingertips, I grasp each strip and uncoil it. The canvas is warped and does not straighten completely. If I force it, the paint will crack and peel. I see evidence that someone has tried to repair the canvas; by the looks of it, again and again. There are layers of glue on the underside, and some miniscule pieces of canvas still stuck to the backing. Whoever repaired this, only to have it destroyed again, took great care to restore it. With humble respect for such devotion, I hold each piece in place as I add new ones, so absorbed in my task I do not even look at the subject until all the pieces are back in place.

I cannot believe what I am seeing.

Neither Beast, nor man.

It is me.

Chapter Six

A festival is taking place in my village today. Like so many times in the past, there will be colorful banners and ribbons streaming from every post. The baker will have his wares laid out on a table in the middle of the square to tempt passers by, and the musicians will stroll through the streets, collecting an eager crowd in their wake.

My father and sisters will be there.

I miss them.

I wonder if they think of me. Do they worry? Have they already forgotten about me? Amalia and Marguerite are of marriageable age now. Have they found suitors yet, or does my absence darken their prospects. As the eldest, I know Marguerite must marry first. But Amalia was always the kinder one.

I worry for my father. Though all of us love him very much, neither Marguerite nor Amalia have ever shown the slightest bit of concern over him.

They do not see the way he sinks into his chair at the close of each day. They do not hear his weary sigh as he hangs his head for a moment before he tugs his boots off his aching feet. My sisters, so concerned about their own looks, do not notice the many wrinkles creasing their beloved father's face, or the gray of his hair.

Monsieur Lafarge gave me his word when I left that he would look after my family in my absence. I can only pray that it is so. The thought that there is no one to care for my father, to cook him stew and make his bed weighs heavily on me. I look around this castle, and guilt falls on my shoulders for being here alone.

They should live in such luxury, not I. I've done nothing to deserve it.

And today, it makes me feel so awfully alone.

The moon is new tonight, and still my Beast has not returned. The servants tell me he has recovered from the poison, but have no answer as to why he still keeps away.

I dream of him nightly. Sometimes I see him as a man, screaming his rage, fighting his bonds like a maddened animal. In those dreams, I feel that if I could just get close to him, if he would just let me, I could calm his fury. I could make him happy.

Other times I see him as my Beast, staring at a picture I cannot see. The look in his eyes is despairing. He is surrounded by beautiful things, and people who love him and wish only the best for him, but he will look at none of them. Only that picture. He looks at it as though he yearns for it desperately, but knows he can never possess it.

That is a strange vision. My Beast is the master of all in this place. It is all his. He has but to ask for something, and it is brought to him on a silver platter. So much wealth and bounty… Why can he not be content?

I sit on the edge of the fountain. The sun shines down brightly, making the water sparkle like diamonds as it falls into the pool. Stone angels stand tall in the middle, other, playful ones sitting and leaning all around them. My gaze turns to the row of trees far in the distance. Beyond it, the road to my village. My home.

I look back at the castle, my new home. I seek out a window high above. The drapes flutter closed and I sigh. He watches me, I know. I will him to come to me, but he does not.

A thought occurs to me; one so horrible I push to my feet and run back inside. Jacques calls after me as I pass him, but I do not slow.

My skirts make me trip on the staircase, but though I bruise my knee, I get up and keep going. My heart races and the stays of my corset feel too tight to take a breath.

The corridor to the Beast's chamber is dark again. I race to the grand portal of his chambers and bang on it with both fists. "Let me in!"

The last time I was here, the man told me I can free one version of him by killing the other. I hit the door harder, and finally kick it. "Is it true?" I demand. "Is that why you're hiding?"

There is no answer.

Tears burn my eyes. I look around for something, anything. The wall sconces are shaped like metal torches. I have to rise up on my toes to wrestle one out of its brace. It is heavy, but makes a satisfyingly loud noise when I bash it against that door. Like the creature behind it, the portal is immovable. But I cannot stop. "You monster! How dare you be afraid of me!"

The door opens and there stands my Beast. He towers over me, his paws as big as my head and claws almost as long as my fingers. Still, he says nothing.

I clutch the torch tighter, though my fingers are cramping. "How could you," I sob, "for even an instant, think I would deliberately do you harm?" *How could you think me such a beast?*

The Beast drops his gaze. It seems he has nothing to say. We stand at an impasse, on either side of the door that can be closed at any moment. We can each pass through and join the other. But we are both rooted in place, some invisible barrier keeping us apart. I want him to meet my gaze and tell me it was a lie. I need him to just look at me and acknowledge my presence. I cannot see inside his mind; have no way of knowing what thoughts swirl behind that fathomless, lost gaze.

And he will not tell me.

I can almost hear the man he turns into, laughing cruelly at his own jest. He has scored a tremendous victory.

I drop the torch and walk away.

Chapter Seven

I can see the carriage emerge from the woods. Though I am smiling, my hands twist in my skirt nervously. That carriage holds everything I cherish in this world: my family.

Jacques announces himself with a knock on the door and, "My lady—"

I rush past him before he can finish. "They're here!"

The servants gawk as I run down to the grand entry hall, but they smile also. It is the first smile I see on their faces since the last full moon. Louis opens the front doors wide and I run outside to greet my father and sisters on the drive, just as they are emerging from the posh carriage.

My father weeps with joy at the sight of me. My sisters embrace me warmly, but their eyes are on the castle and its grounds. They've never seen such grandeur before. I take them inside and show them where I've been spending my days. I give each of them the same warning the Beast first gave me: Do not enter the west wing. They nod, but when I turn my back, I can see in the great mirror in front of me my sisters exchanging a conspiratorial look.

Jacques sees it also. He inclines his head to me in a silent message. He will keep my sisters away from where they ought not be. I am grateful for his vigilance.

When at last I have shown them all there is to see, I leave my family in the capable hands of the maids. They will show my father and sisters to their rooms and make certain they have everything they need.

"A successful welcome, if I may say so," Jacques says. He is courteous and obliging as always, but I can sense he is happy for me. These last few days have not been easy on me. Having been shunned by the very man I am meant to save, I thought about running away. So many times I came to the doorway with my cloak about my shoulders, only to stop. I am the greatest of fools. Even after everything, I still cannot abandon him.

But that does not mean I will tolerate his treatment of me in silence. I smile, and it feels genuine. "It was, indeed. I take it as a good sign that they've not run screaming yet."

"Well, perhaps that will come later."

Despite myself, I laugh. "Do not dare jest about such things."

Jacques bows to hide his smile. "My apologies, Lady Lyssette. I am sure the master will be on his best behavior."

I hope so. My father has already seen the master of this castle before, and it speaks highly of his bravery, and his love for me that he came back. My sisters, on the other hand, have no prior knowledge of the Beast. And I fear their curiosity will lead to their ruin. "See that he is," I tell Jacques playfully. "Or he and I shall have to have words about it."

Jacques chuckles on his way out. As he opens the door, Marguerite straightens guiltily. I can tell from the blush staining her cheeks that she was eavesdropping. Jacques prudently says nothing; pretends he does not see her.

"Come in, please."

Marguerite drags her feet into the parlor, looking around. "So this is where you were. And to think Father was so terribly worried about his little girl Lyssette."

There is bitterness in her voice. It should have been Marguerite, not me. That was the agreement our father said he struck with the Beast. A single rose cut from his gardens, my father's life and freedom, in exchange for his eldest daughter. Marguerite would be living here now, had I not run away to take her place instead.

"Looks can be deceiving. Perhaps Father was right to worry."

Marguerite picks up a candlestick. It is made of solid gold. "I am sure," she says.

Perhaps, before emerging onto the beautifully tended grounds, Marguerite worried also. Perhaps she even felt a little gratitude to me, for having spared her the horrid fate of being a Beast's prisoner. What must she think of me now? And of our father! Does she think him deluded? Senile in his old age, to have said he saw a great and terrible beast within this castle?

I try not to think too much about that. "Tell me of home. Has Monsieur Lafarge offered his patronage?"

"Oh, of course he has. He comes by every week to see if we've everything we need. And he never forgets to ask about you. *And how is Lyssette? When is she expected back?* He expects you to marry him, you know."

Surprise makes me startle. *Marry* him?

"He's made no secret of it. The entire village is talking about it. The great wedding of Monsieur Lafarge and the pauper Lyssette. The children are all dutifully on the lookout for Cinderlyssette's lost glass slipper."

My heart races and my cheeks flush. I feel overheated. Somehow I make it to the plush seat by the window and lower myself into it. Monsieur Lafarge is three times my age, if not more. He is also the richest man in our village, though compared to the master of this castle, he himself might be called a pauper.

When I asked him to look after my family, I never intended for his help to be in coin. And I certainly never imagined this was how he would want that debt repaid. My God, what have I gotten myself into now? What would Monsieur Lafarge do if I refused him? He could ruin us.

Marguerite smiles acidly. "Did you really think you'd find your happy ending by running away from the life you were meant for?"

Chapter Eight

"You're not marrying him."

I've no idea when or how the Beast appeared in the parlor, but he is here now, glaring at the door Marguerite just closed behind her. "Finally, you decide to come out of hiding."

His mouth pulls away from his big, sharp teeth. "There are... people in my home," he says. "I don't like it. And you're not marrying him."

I never intended to, but I do not feel merciful enough to tell him so now. "I might not have a choice. You heard my sister, Monsieur Lafarge has gone to great lengths to take care of my family in my absence and—"

"Lafarge is a bilious, tight fisted wretch. He was a bastard fifty years ago, and he is still a bastard now. You are not marrying him."

How does he know that? My heart squeezes at the reminder of his curse. Now I have a sense of how long it must have lasted. He must have known the man in his youth. The Lafarge family was always rich. Ever since they laid claim to the largest fields. They owned the majority of farmland and employed the villagers to do the work, selling them back the fruits of the land. Because most of the food comes from his farms, Monsieur Jean Lafarge, as the last surviving heir now holds the village in the palm of his hand.

"Whom should I marry instead?" I ask softly.

The Beast's feral gaze turns on me, blue eyes blazing with jealous fury. But he does not offer an alternative. He takes a deep breath and exhales it on a growl of annoyance. "Why did you not tell me your family needed help?"

"And what would you have done, if I had?" The Beast was and still is a solitary creature. He tolerates the servants, because they are just as bound by the curse as he. And he tolerates my presence because… because I am the only hope he has left. But he cannot risk allowing others into his demesne. Even the presence of my family could be dangerous. Should they decide to run screaming back to the village, the Beast would have an army of scared, angry villagers at his door, carrying pitch forks and torches.

No, he and I both know that he would not have done anything. Because he cannot expose himself.

"I would have found a way," he says.

That is more than I expected. But too late, nonetheless. "Thank you."

He lowers his great frame to the floor, sits at my feet and lays his great head in my lap. "I missed you," he says.

"You did not have to."

"Lyssette, are you happy here with me?"

"Now that my father and sisters are here, I am. I pretend that this is all there is, and that we can all stay here forever, and everything will turn out well."

He raises his head to look at me. "Why pretend?"

"Because I am coming to realize that I am not here to save you. All I can do is help you save yourself."

"Even if that were true, it doesn't make me need you any less."

There is that desperate look in his eyes again, like a lost child looking for his mother. Without him telling me, I know he fears I will leave. I want to reassure him, but the truth is I do not know what will happen. When the curse is broken, and all the world is his to explore again, he won't need me anymore. Will he even notice if I leave then? Will he miss me, even a little?

My heart says yes. But my head doubts. I have seen the Beast at his absolute worst now. I've felt like I was fighting a lost battle. He is holding back from me; even after all these months he still does not trust me completely.

"I am not going anywhere," I say. And for now, at least, it is the truth.

Chapter Nine

Tonight is the first night of the full moon. The Beast and I both dread it. Though I have not told him, my father senses the danger. He does not worry only for me. As my sisters get used to their new surroundings they grow bolder each day.

Marguerite already took to ordering the servants around. She works her lady's maid like a slave and I pity the poor girl for having been dealt that cruel hand. I know Jacqueline will never tell me, but I suspect Marguerite has struck her a time or two.

Amalia is the curious one. She already found one of the ruined portraits of the Beast and ran screaming from the castle. She was not frightened, merely starved for attention. I worry that she will wander where she ought not. The Beast will not take kindly to such a trespass.

And tonight, of all nights, Marguerite requested a family feast. Naturally she expects our host to join us. I was never so ashamed of my own sister as I was yesterday, when in a lofty tone she told

Jacques that his master's presence was welcome at his own dinner table, where his own food would be served.

Now I look at my own reflection, and a lovely woman draped in a beautiful gown looks back at me worriedly wringing her hands. I know this night will end in some sort of disaster. Marguerite is not kind to those who spurn her.

Jacques enters after a polite knock. "My lady, your family awaits you in the grand dining room."

"Tell me truthfully, Jacques, do you regret letting them in the front door?"

"My lady, I am merely grateful that I let you in," he says with a perfect bow.

Despite my worry, I smile. "Thank you, Jacques. For every kindness you have shown me and my family."

A few more moments of fussing and I am ready as I shall ever be to face Marguerite's wrath. The sun has gone down. At this very moment, the man she is so eager to meet is chained to the floor of his empty chamber. He will know of our presence and I've no doubt he will be maddened. And tomorrow night I shall have to go face him.

I take a bracing breath and step out of the safety of my room into the hallway.

No!

The shock of what I see stops me in my tracks.

He's here!

Not chained in his chamber. Certainly not raging impotently at another intrusion into his home. The monster of a man the gentle Beast turns into is coming down the hallway, dressed for a party and adjusting his cravat!

I feel my heart racing in my throat and cannot take a breath. My face feels cold, leeched of all blood at the sight of him. How can this be? How could he have possibly broken free?

He sees me and a malicious grin spreads across his handsome, cold face. I back away as he advances, but not fast enough. He reaches me before I can escape and catches my arm in a painful grip. "Hello, little bird," he says at my ear.

"W-what are you doing here?" Despite my best efforts, my voice quivers. I cannot be strong when fear courses through me like Death's whisper.

"Isn't it obvious? I have been invited to dinner, and that is precisely where I intend to be tonight." He tugs on my arm to make me turn. It hurts enough that I am forced to obey. "Come, let me look at what I must wear on my arm."

I hold still while his gaze moves over me in disgusting appraisal.

"I suppose you'll have to do," he says. Judgment passed. "Now come, we don't want to keep our guests waiting, do we?"

I gasp. "No!" He is already pulling me toward the staircase. I dig in my heels to slow him down. "Don't, please! Stop!"

"You will address me as 'My lord.' I suppose you'll have to use my name if we're to pretend we know each other." His tone implies a very intimate sort of knowledge. I have no time to be offended. "Call me 'My Lord Bastien,' then."

"Please—"

He stops and whirls about so quickly I slam into him. His chest is hard and unyielding as rock and I know the heart that beats within is cold as ice when he looks into my wide eyes and says, "Please, what?"

I know he is not asking what I want from him. I swallow my pride for the sake of my family and answer, "Please, my Lord Bastien."

"Mmm, I like the sound of that."

"What," I say before I can stop myself, "the sound of your own name?"

"The sound of you begging."

"You cannot go down there." No matter what my condition, if he enters the same room as my father and sisters, there will be a fight. I cannot allow that.

He laughs at me. "And what's to stop me? You?" The laughter dies away. "You…" With another appraising look he releases my arm and circles me. "You wish me to abstain from the company of your dear father and delightful sisters?"

"Yes," I say, enduring his perusal.

"And what would you give me in return?"

"What do you want?"

"Ah-ah."

My hands curl into fists at my sides. "What do you want, my Lord Bastien?"

"Better." He stops behind me and there is silence. If it were not for his breath on my shoulder, I would think he left. "You will come to my chambers tomorrow night."

"Why?"

"Do you wish your family to dine in peace tonight?"

"Yes," I hiss.

"Then you'll do as I say. Your brooding monster of a hero cannot save you this time, little bird. I am free and he'll not restrain me again. *I am your master now, and you will do what I say when I say.* Is that clear?"

I hesitate just long enough.

"Or perhaps we should join the others. It's quite unseemly to be so dreadfully late to dinner."

Helpless tears fill my eyes. "I will do as you say… my Lord Bastien."

"Now there's a good pet. Run along now, your guests are waiting."

"What will you do?"

He does not answer. When I turn around, he is gone.

Chapter Ten

There are no guards in front of the door. But the hallway is, for the first time, lit with a dozen wall sconces. It is bright enough to be day, though it is close to midnight. I lick my lips nervously. Just as on that night months ago, I feel like a sacrifice willingly walking to her demise. My palms are moist and my limbs tremble. I know there will be no chains to hold him back tonight. A spurned master, he will want to take his revenge.

He warned me this day would come. But I've grown so complacent, so trusting that my Beast would never harm me that I chose not to believe him. More fool I.

I raise my hand to knock but the door opens before I can rap even once. "You kept me waiting," Bastien drawls as his gaze sweeps over me in a thorough perusal.

"I—"

"I don't care." He grasps my wrist and pulls me inside, closing the door behind me. But he remains in place, trapping me between him and the portal at my back. I shrink back from the terrible light in his eyes. He is not wearing the Beast's tattered remains of clothing, nor is he clad in a crisp suit like last night. Tonight he is shirtless, and infinitely more intimidating because of it. He has no shame; his intent is to humiliate me.

"What do you want from me?"

He sneers. "What do you think I want?"

I lick my dry lips. His gaze snares on them. "I'm sure I have no idea."

He shoves away and turns his back on me. The candlelight makes his muscles stand out even more. Such strength and power. So much energy and life. So much rage and cruelty imprisoned in that body. "You will stay the whole night," he says.

"But—"

"Too late to turn back now, my pretty. You and I have a deal."

"And how can I be sure you will honor your part of it?"

He looks back at me, his blue eyes mocking. "I suppose you will have to take it on faith. And what have I told you about using my name?"

"I'll make a bargain with you."

In the blink of an eye he is upon me. His hands dig into my arms as he hauls me deeper into his lair and shoves me against the wall. "You are in no position to bargain," he snarls.

"I disagree," I say. I cannot tell where the courage to do so comes from but the words do not stop until I have said my peace. "You need me. I have something you want. I am the only one who can set you free."

He bares his teeth, livid and quivering. His fingers dig in more and I stifle a wince.

"So you and I *will* bargain. Or I walk out of here forever and leave you to enjoy the rest of eternity. Three nights at a time."

"I will skin you alive, you little bitch."

"What you will do is release me. Now."

To my utter shock, he does. With a final shove that bruises my back, he lets go of me and steps back, glaring as though he would like nothing better than to follow through on his threat. And I realize that I am not completely powerless in this exchange. I've allowed my fear to rule me, blind me to everything I should have been paying attention to.

This man before me is a clever, calculating monster. But he is also crazed by his confinement and so desperate to escape it any way he can that, like me, he is blinded to what is right in front of him.

I draw a cautious breath and square my shoulders. I am finished with him tonight. I turn toward the door.

"Not so fast," he says. Then he is at my back, leaning in to me. He does not touch me, but his mouth is right at my ear when he speaks again, and his hot breath tickles. "You might be a necessary bane… but your family is not." He moves to speak in my other ear. "So our bargain still holds, mistress. You will do as I say tonight. *Everything* I say. Or I pay them a long overdue visit."

My heart sinks. The proud set of my shoulders slumps a little and my head bows in defeat. "What do you intend for me to do… my Lord Bastien?"

His arm comes around me and there is a book in his hand. "I intend for you to read," he says mockingly.

I take the book from him and he retreats. The light is too dim in here. I will have to enter his bed chamber to see well enough to read. When I face it, he is already lounging insolently on the grand bed someone has brought in. He reminds me of a spoiled sheikh in a long ago story. One so sure of himself and his claim to rule that he does not care for anything or anyone.

He watches me come into the room, a satisfied gleam in his eyes. "Over there," he says, indicating a chaise near the brightest light. It is the same one I used a month ago to read to him, when he would hear none of it. Now he demands the written words. And the chaise is not as I remember it. It is draped with silks and there are pillows placed on it.

I sit. The title of the book is not familiar to me. I open it to the first page and begin reading. "*Chapter One. The first woman I have ever lain with had…*"

"Go on," he says and I can hear the laughter in his voice. I dare not look up. My eyes skim ahead on the page and my cheeks flush. "She had… what?"

I squeeze my eyes shut. My hands tremble holding the book.

"Read," he orders.

"The first woman I have ever lain with," I start again, drawing breath for strength to continue, "had t-tits that could smother a man. They overflowed my hands when I held them and sucked until she screamed like a stuck pig. Her name was Annabel, the best whore money could buy…"

I read the words and do not allow myself to think of them. The book is crudely written and difficult to decipher. But what it describes is far, far worse. Lewd descriptions of one man's love affairs, every detail penned in heavy hand. Down to the color of a woman's nipples and how she felt around his member.

And all the while I read Bastien watches me in silence. He never stirs, never speaks, merely observes my humiliation; revels in it. Every so often my concentration breaks and I comprehend what it is I am reading. I stutter and choke on the words, pausing for long moments in hopes that he will take pity on me and allow me to stop.

He does not. He makes me read until the very end. Every last sordid word. When I finish, I snap the book shut and throw it on the ground. I would never treat a proper book this way. This one is an abomination. An insult to the written word.

"Well done, Lyssette," Bastien mocks.

"You disgust me."

He chuckles. "Do I?"

"How could you possibly enjoy this? How could a man write such things?"

"So innocent." He says it as an insult.

I cannot even look at him. My humiliation runs too deep. If I meet his gaze now, I know I will not be able to control myself. I do not know which would be worse: to burst into tears before him, or attack him. I know his strength is far superior to mine, and I know he would merely enjoy the sight of my tears so much more.

"Come back tomorrow night. I have something else for you to read."

"Are we finished?" I ask stiffly. He demanded I stay the night. It is not yet morning, though the sun will be coming up any moment.

"For now," he says. I can still sense his eyes on me. It makes me feel unclean. I push to my feet and walk out of the chamber without looking at him. "Good day, Lyssette," he calls after me.

I would slam the door behind me but the sight of Marguerite out in the hallway stops me cold. "What are you doing here?"

Marguerite shakes her head with disgust. "You little whore," she says.

Her words make resentment coil inside me. "You were told not to come here."

"Yes, and now I can see why. So where is your lover? No need to hide him now. Or do you exhaust him so completely that he has no strength left to see his guests?"

Before I can utter a cutting remark, a scream carries from inside the chamber. It saps what little strength I have left. My heart aches for the Beast. Because I know I am failing him. Every time he endures that transformation is pain he should not be feeling any longer. He should be free by now. Why can I not free him?

Marguerite's eyes widen. "My God, Lyssette, what have you done to him?" She shoves past me to the door.

"Marguerite, don't!"

But I am too late to stop her. She bursts into the chamber, heading straight for the suffering Beast. I follow on her heels and we both stop when the screaming stops and the Beast drops to his hands and knees. He is breathing hard, low growls rumbling in his chest. I cannot see Marguerite's face but I hear her gasp and I can tell she's stopped breathing.

My Beast lifts his great head, his weary eyes alighting on the two of us. He growls, hackles rising. "*Get out!*" he roars so loud the walls shudder.

Marguerite screams and runs. No doubt she will wake the entire castle with her hysterics. I should be more concerned, but I am tired. I help the shivering Beast up and to his bed we do not even look at each other and by the time he is settled I am so weary I can barely stand.

Marguerite is gone, the servants must be up already, and my family will soon be asking them many questions. I curl up at the foot of the grand bed and allow sleep to claim me. Consequences be damned.

Chapter Eleven

Sounds invade my dreams. A familiar voice speaks my name. I hear it calling but my mind is too weary to rouse.

"No," I hear. "Let her sleep."

A warm blanket settles over me and I sigh. I didn't realize I was so cold.

Then strange dreams once more pull me away into an unknown land. I see statues weeping. They come to life before my very eyes, reaching out to me. Wolves howl in the distant forest, taunting and jeering. They are closing in and I know this time there is no iron gate to keep them out. They near swiftly and they are coming for me.

I wake with a start. Candles are lit everywhere and the windows are wide open to let in the evening air. This is not my chamber. How long have I been asleep?

"Ah, the beauty wakes."

There is my answer: long enough that the sun already went down and it is no gentle beast sitting on the bed behind me.

"I was beginning to think you'd sleep through the night." Someone freed my hair while I slept. He eases it to the side now, exposing my shoulder. His lips brush over my skin. "I would not have minded."

I shove away from him, desperate to escape his hold and his bed. He catches my arm and pulls me back. We struggle but it is no more than a game to him. He laughs at my feeble attempts to get away from him. His much stronger body pins me beneath him. His hands capture mine so easily. I am trapped, left to his mercy—and I already know he has none.

We stare at each other, his heavy lidded eyes reflecting the candle light all around. His weight on me makes it difficult to breathe. Still, I suck in air to scream. Surely someone is nearby. Surely they will be brave enough to oppose their master and rescue me.

He silences me swiftly. "Ah-ah now, little bird. None of that. You'll only worry our guests."

"Let me go," I say, unable to disguise the fear in my voice.

"We have a bargain."

"For me to read to you. Not... do *this*."

"Yes, well, that was before you availed yourself of my bed for an afternoon nap. I've decided to amend the terms slightly."

"No."

He merely smiles. "Don't you want to know what I've come up with?" He leans his face into my neck and inhales deeply. "Mm, I thought it was quite generous, given our... unusual circumstances."

"I'm sure you did. The answer is still no."

"Well then," he says, levering himself up, "it's high time you got out of bed. We've guests to attend to. They've already been asking about you." He releases me and I fight and tug on the tangle of skirts and sheets to escape to freedom.

"I won't stay here another minute. I'm leaving and taking my family with me." The moment I am on my feet, I run for the door. I just manage to open it when he slams it shut again with one hand. His speed amazes me. His strength is frightening.

"You needn't bother," he murmurs in my ear. "I've already instructed the guards to bar the gate. They will not dare disobey me. *No one* leaves the castle until I say so."

"You're keeping us prisoner?"

He pries my hand away from the handle and turns me to face him. "That's one way to think of it."

"Damn you!"

He throws his head back and laughs. "Oh, my sweet Lyssette. I'm already damned."

His new terms are scandalous. As he'd said last night, he has a new book for me to read, and this one is far worse than the last. It is written by a woman. This time, he insists I sit on the bed with him. I refuse, of course, but in the end he gives me no choice. The one concession I am able to extract from him is that he will not touch me.

To my surprise, he grants another, which I have not thought to ask. Moments after I agree to these new terms there is a knock on the door. He answers it himself and I prepare myself for another scene like the one last night. I will not be able to explain my presence here, or my absence all day long. And with Bastien in his human form, I will not be able to explain what Marguerite saw this morning.

But when Bastien opens the door there is no one on the other side. There is only a trolley laden with covered dishes. He brings it inside. "Don't get excited," he tells me, "*He* did this, not me."

We dine together. As there are no chairs or tables, we are forced to sit close enough to bump elbows every time one of us reaches for something. He does not say a word but I can see by his expression how much he enjoys the feast. From what my beast told me, Bastien has not had a proper meal in a very long time.

But dinner is over too soon and then I've no more excuses. Now sated, Bastien seems almost in good spirits. He does not rush me or make any more demands. I would be grateful, except I know why he is so calm and complacent. He set the terms and I agreed. He might have opened the door, but he will make certain I walk through it all on my own.

I move all the way to the foot of the bed, as far from him as I can possibly get. The book lies ready between us. I pick it up and steady my nerves. "*Memoires of Madame Bordeaux*," the title reads. I open the volume to the first page. There is a dedication penned in an elegant hand: "*To my Lord Bastien, with fond memories of the nights we spent together, and covetous wishes for more.*" I look up at him. "This woman was your lover."

He smiles. "Yes."

"And she gave you a book of accounts of all her other lovers?"

"I believe she gave one to all her acquaintances. She was quite proud of her writing and, as you'll see, not shy about her profession."

"I cannot believe that—"

"You will. Once you read it you'll see how you've been deceived all your life."

"Deceived?"

"You've been taught that sex is merely the means by which humans beget children."

"And is it not?"

"It's not all it is. It is quite enjoyable. A pastime I indulged in often when I was myself. Now that monstrous bastard has made a monk of me." He takes a strawberry from the tray and bites into it. "A *hungry* monk."

I am coming to understand how Bastien's mind works. He despises me for my prudence and what he called innocence. Any attempt to change him from his wicked ways would only invite scorn. My only recourse is to stoop to his level and be just as wicked.

"I would not be surprised if the reason for your curse was your inability to keep your cock in your pants," I say. Though my words are daring, my face burns with an embarrassed flush. I've never said such a thing before. Then again, I've never known about such things until last night.

Bastien laughs. I've shocked him. Even amused him. He does not reply, merely shakes his head. I am heartened that he does not make jest of me and even smile as I turn the page. "*Chapter one,*" I read. "*There is an art to making love, which many men, but few women understand. Whereas a man can avail himself of any means to his own pleasure, a woman is to make do with what she's been allotted, something a man rarely appreciates. I find this reprehensible.* Hmm, I like her already. *Bringing his woman pleasure in bed is the very least a man ought to do for his wife or lover. I consider it my greatest life achievement that I was able to tutor so many fine men into attentive, expert lovers…*"

Chapter Twelve

Change is a concept I have become very familiar with. I thought by now I would have embraced it, learned it is a natural part of life. Yet to say that I have become used to it would be to belie the concept. If one becomes used to change, then nothing truly changes them.

The truth is I've not gotten used to it at all.

The truth is my Beast is not the only one changing.

It is difficult to think of myself now as having once been that sure footed girl with a book always in hand, who never knew a moment's hesitation. That girl, that innocent—and I can see now just how innocent she truly was—is disappearing little by little every day. I cannot say with certainty that it is wholly Bastien's doing.

Nothing is the same in this ever perfect, ever cursed castle. When servants whisper now, it is with scandalized excitement. For the first time in a very long time, they have something to gossip about. It seems that is enough to put smiles on their faces. Every duty they perform these days they do with joy. I even hear them singing sometimes.

My family, too, is different. Marguerite is gone. Jacques tells me she ran away that night and has not returned. He's sent a messenger to our village in disguise to seek her out. Thankfully, she's made it home unharmed. Jacques assures me she is well, if a little unsettled. With the eldest away, Amalia is flourishing. She spends most of her time in the grand ballroom where Francois teaches her to dance. Perhaps in another time, another place, Amalia was meant to be a princess. Dancing becomes her.

Father is not so easily distracted. Though he smiles at me and speaks with me the way he used to, there is a heaviness in his gaze. He strolls in the gardens and his shoulders seem weighted down. I ask him to confide in me but he waves my worries away, smiles, and tells me he loves me. He is not easy here, I know. It must unnerve him, sleeping in the lair of the beast, knowing that one of his daughters is bound to him. And now with Marguerite gone...

Aimee let slip today that Father went to see my Beast. He's never done that before, not willingly. Aimee will not tell me what they spoke about, even though I am certain she must have overheard. Father and the Beast will not tell me, either. Both deny having spoken at all.

My monthly visits with Bastien are making me paranoid. Whenever I catch my thoughts straying more toward the ridiculous, I go to the library to read. But these days my hand reaches not for the works of Homer, Virgil, Socrates, and Dante, but the more obscure names, oft times scrawled across the book's cover with a quill and chafed almost clean off.

What I read in these volumes can hardly compare to the classics. It is crudely worded and poorly written but this lack of polish reveals stories far truer than any poem from Rome. Rather than pretty, they are heartfelt. Letters and passages recounting lives filled with love, hate, envy, greed, pain, suffering, and incredible joy. I read about men going out into the world to make their fortune. About the wives and children they leave behind.

I read these things and they shock me with their poignancy. So much raw emotion, written into books by people whose lives were distinguished not by grand deeds of heroism or martyrdom, but by the silent tears they wept late at night when no one would see them. By the heartsick sighs hidden behind sociable smiles, while their coveted love flirted with another. By the cries of joy torn from them in those secret moments shared with their lover.

I seek out these book because I crave those feelings I've hardly experienced. I've never felt love so deep it cut me to the quick. I've never known anguish so great I thought to end it by my own hand. Though I've felt joy, it has always been tempered by other things.

It shames me to admit that the stories which captivate me most are ones of passion.

The very books I've blushed over in Bastien's chamber are ones I have read again and again, seeking meaning in the minutest details. I can hardly admit even to myself that more and more now I steal away from company to hide where no one will see me read such shocking things. Though I am careful, always keeping a proper book at hand, I'm afraid I could not tear my gaze away from those pages even long enough to cover my indiscretion. I would not even notice anyone nearby.

This is how I while away the time until the moon rises full again. I tell myself it is merely to be prepared, so that next time I will not blush so fiercely to read such things aloud. I tell myself that if I can only show Bastien that his tactics no longer shock me, we can find some common ground.

I tell myself anything I must to justify taking the next book off the shelf.

I read until I am too tired to make out the words, and fall asleep with the book still in my hands. What the writers have begun, my mind continues in sleep. I dream of things that cannot be put into words. It is as though I am the one living those things, wholeheartedly engaging in one lurid act or another.

I dream of being kissed so deeply that breath becomes secondary. Of being stripped of my gown and watched by a burning, lustful gaze. I dream of hands caressing my skin and sifting through my hair. At times I can feel lips on mine, hot breath searing me. My heartbeat quickens at such dreams and I awake in a tangle of sheets, overheated and a little frightened. I fight to catch my breath and dread falling asleep once more, but eventually I always do.

And he is always there, waiting for me to return to him. His insatiable eyes roam over me; his words are gruff praise that makes me shiver. I long for him to take me in his arms again. My body aches without him. I've never felt such things before and cannot seem to control them. They overwhelm me until, if he does not come to me,

I rush to him and cover his face with kisses, pleading. For what, I do not know.

From the welling tension, I jar awake crying his name: "Bastien!"

I have, indeed, changed.

I am no longer the same Lyssette who boldly walked through the gate and stood before the raging beast, daring him to claim his demanded prize.

I am the wiser, foolish one who would run through the doors and throw herself at the cruel man, begging him to do so.

Chapter Thirteen

Amalia has another new gown. The expensive blue silk with silver ribbon trimming is the most extravagant thing I've ever seen. It shimmers in the light, like ocean waves. Noelle beams, watching Amalia twirl about. She is quite proud of the work she's done on the gown. It flatters Amalia, just like all the other gowns do.

"Isn't it wonderful, Lys?"

"Indeed."

"Have you ever seen anything so beautiful?"

"I have not," I say.

"You look stunning, Mademoiselle."

"And don't I look like a princess?"

Neither I nor Noelle have an answer for this but Amalia doesn't mind or notice. She laughs in delight and twirls in front of the gilded mirror she ordered to be brought for her. "I want one just like this in every colour!"

Noelle looks at me aghast but I shake my head, assuring her that no more gowns will be necessary for Amalia's ever growing wardrobe.

Amalia screams in terror, shocking us to our feet. Heart racing out of control I look to see what frightened her so. Pale faced, frozen to the spot, my sister stares into the mirror. It is not her own reflection that scared her so. In the long shadows of dying day, close to the floor on all fours glowers the Beast.

He bares his teeth at the noise, his fur rising in agitation, but he does not growl. Nor, however, does he disappear as he is wont to.

"God preserve us," Amalia whispers, crossing herself.

Now the surly beast growls. "God?" He slinks forward a step, just enough to come into the light. I've seen that fierce look in his eyes before. Something must have angered him enough to come out of hiding. "God did not make me this way. He did not lift a finger to preserve *me*. Why should he bother to spare you?"

"L-Lys?"

"It's all right, Amalia. Noelle, if you'd be so kind, please take my sister to her rooms now. I'm sure there are still adjustments to be done before dinner time."

"Yes, my lady." Noelle curtsies and herds the gawking Amalia out of the ballroom. I am once again left alone with my Beast and he is in a temper.

"Useless wastrel," he growls, staring after Amalia.

I am offended at this and want to rally to Amalia's defense. My sister has always liked pretty things but she's never spent a coin she could not afford to part with. Yet as I think back, I remember her obsession with balls and village celebrations. She's always loved adoring crowds and the revelry they brought with them.

True, she never spent more than she could afford but her coin was spent on ribbons and paste jewels. Amalia always dreamed about being a princess. Now, here, she can finally pretend she is one. I could not deny her that for anything. But my Beast does not share my affection for her—and it is *his* castle she plays pretend in, *his* coin she spends on new gowns.

I have no excuse for her behavior. "At least she didn't run screaming out of the castle," I say, suddenly feeling like an unwanted guest whose presence must be tolerated.

The Beast grunts. "I think I would prefer if she did."

I recognize that change in his voice. For a creature so used to solitude I begin to suspect he enjoys our presence here. I can only attribute his inexplicable appearance now to a desire to make himself part of our family gatherings.

I smile and his eyes soften. "I prefer your gown to hers," he says.

The compliment is gruff, unpracticed, but genuine. I incline my head and curtsy. "Thank you, my lord."

His gaze moves past me to the window and the gathering dusk outside. "Full moon tonight."

"Yes," I say.

He expects me to say more, but I can think of nothing to add. We both know what nightfall will bring. My Beast knows far better than I what will await me tonight. His eyes turn bleak. "Am I losing you, Lyssette?"

I am taken aback by his question. "N-no. Of course not!" If anything I am more dedicated to my quest to free him.

He says nothing, merely searches my face for answers to questions he is too afraid to ask. Then he turns and disappears soundlessly back into the shadows.

Perturbed, I retire to my chambers to dress for dinner. My mind returns time and again to his words. *Am I losing you, Lyssette?* What could he mean by that?

I bathe and dress in the gown I had Jocelyn air out for me earlier. I need her help to fasten it; the row of buttons running down the back is intricate and difficult to do without seeing. When she is finished, she helps me arrange my hair in flattering curls. I leave it loose tonight, knowing I will be too tired later to take out any pins and will only stab myself with them when I lie down to sleep.

The gown is a beautiful, dark green silk with white embroidery and lace trimmings, like snow covering the forest canopy. It makes the green in my eyes stand out, not quite the jewel emerald of Jocelyn's, but softer, warmed by the brown of my father's. "Thank you, Jocelyn," I say, smiling at my reflection.

"You look beautiful, my lady."

"All thanks to you."

"Not at all, my lady," Jocelyn says. "You've a natural beauty few women have. Even the lord said so."

I have heard the servants talking often enough to know that they address only Bastien by the title 'lord.' The Beast they refer to as 'master.' Surprised for the second time tonight, I can think of nothing to say.

Jocelyn's cheeks turn pink. She must realize what she said. She mumbles something about chores, dips a quick curtsy and leaves in a hurry. I bring a gloved hand to my own heated cheeks. The man I called monster has never had a kind word for me, in the six nights I have spent with him. Is this another of his tricks? When could Jocelyn have overheard him saying a thing like that?

The sun winks at me in the mirror as the last of its rays dull. Sunset. I grasp my skirts and hasten to the door. I want to be there when Bastien transforms. Better I find him than he seeks me out. Though the Beast is becoming more amenable toward my family, I would not trust Bastien within a furlong of them.

I pull the door open and stifle a startled gasp to find the Beast waiting on the other side. He looks me over from the curls of my hair, down to my gown and slippered feet. His eyes dim somewhat. "You dressed for him," he says.

The first spasm hits him before I can say anything. He lurches forward and I move quickly out of the way as the pain makes him fall to the floor. He bites back the screams but his anguished moans break my heart. I close the door so that the others might not hear. He crawls to the bed as his body changes in sickening breaks and shifts. One large paw grasps the edge of the mattress, shredding the covering even as his claws turn to human fingers.

I watch in silence, unable to help, wanting desperately to see the curse finally end somehow. When it is over, Bastien levers himself up. He stands on unsteady legs, keeping hold of the tall bed for balance as he catches his breath. His clothes now hang on him, made for the Beast and much too large on him. Even so, the body draped in a wrinkled white shirt and tattered black pants is anything but small or weak.

When he turns to me, he is once again perfectly all right, if a little winded. His eyes flicker from cold annoyance to burning lust as he looks me over. "Ah," he says, his mouth pulling into a mocking sneer. "You dressed for me."

Chapter Fourteen

"You shouldn't have," Bastien drawls.

"I didn't," I retort, though after the Beast's accusation, I cannot be sure. I did not intentionally choose a gown to please Bastien. That it does makes me feel as though I am deceiving the Beast.

"I would have much preferred you without the gown."

He does not come closer but his gaze is piercing enough that I back myself against the closed door. Oh, how pathetically I cower before this man. I dreamed of him night after night. I imagined scenes so lurid I could hardly admit them aloud. I was brave in those visions, boldly meeting him in kind. Where has that bravery gone now that he is flesh and blood before me?

My heart beats so loud in the quiet room I am afraid he will hear. I do not rise to his bait and he does not press it. He merely gazes at me, as if the sight pleases him. His silent perusal is far more unsettling than anything he might say.

He comes a step closer but no more. "I had intricate plans for this night," he says, tracing the embroidery on my bodice with his gaze. I can almost feel it as a physical caress. I press my back harder against the door to disguise my shiver. It unsettles me to be looked at with such unabashed hunger, but not nearly as much as it ought to. It does not scare me.

It should. Bastien can hurt me in ways I cannot even imagine; not even after having fallen asleep two months ago with his shouted threats still echoing through my mind. Not even after all those books I've read.

"Elaborate preparations, plots within plots, and all that." He comes another step closer; close enough to touch but he does not reach out. My gloved fingers dig into the door at my back. Better that than his chest. I want to push him away. I want to pull him closer. "But now I think this is much better. A prettily wrapped present just for me."

Bastien braces his hands on the door on either side of me, caging me in. He leans closer, dragging his gaze up from my chest to my eyes. "You're trembling," he murmurs, satisfaction shining in his blue eyes. "Do I frighten you?"

Yes! I want to scream. Instead, my lips whisper, "No."

I surprised him. He accepts my words as a challenge. Shifting his weight, he frees one hand and takes hold of a strand of my hair, looping it around his finger. "You would not be so brave if you could see what I am thinking."

I swallow with difficulty. Bastien's eyes note the action, stare at my neck. He releases my hair and moves the curls over my shoulder to bare more of it. I know he can see my pulse fluttering because I can *feel* it. I tense as he leans closer still, breathing in deep close to my skin. I grow light headed, my knees become weak. I've read about this in the books. It is the part where the woman grasps onto the man and he puts his arms about her, taking her weight when she can no longer stand on her own.

I know Bastien will do no such thing. I must rely on the door to steady me.

"You've let him do this—get close enough to have your scent, taste your skin. I felt you tremble with fear of him. You don't smell of fear now, Lyssette."

Do not ask! "What do you smell, then?" The words tumble out on a whisper of breath rushing past my lips. I cannot keep my breathing even any longer. I can smell *him* now. He carries the scent of the forest on his skin, earth and grass, and something I cannot even describe. I want to breathe him in as he did me.

He inhales again and his lips brush over my shoulder. "Heat," he says. "Prim and proper, pretty Mademoiselle Lyssette. A siren's lure. You could burn me alive if I'm not careful."

I could burn *myself*. I already feel heat pooling in my belly. My blood runs like liquid fire through my veins. The silk gown is too thick, too heavy. It is suffocating me. I want to rip it off so that I might take a full breath.

I can feel him smile against my neck. "You've impressed me. The last woman who read my books to me begged me to take her before she was even finished. I took great pleasure in reading every last word to her until she came apart in my arms."

My body tenses at his words, even as my legs become weaker still. "I… I can't breathe," I gasp out.

He turns me around so fast my head spins. I press my cheek against the cool door, seeking relief from this infernal heat but it will not abate. Bastien tugs my hair away from my nape and his teeth nip me lightly as he sets to work on the buttons of my gown. With each one that comes loose I can breathe a little easier. The garment sags on my arms. If I just lower them it will slide to the floor to pool at my feet.

"I could make you beg so easily," he whispers at my ear. "But I'd rather hear you scream."

I cry out as he snatches me up into his arms. With two steps we are by the bed and he tosses me onto it. The covers billow around me and before they settle, Bastien is upon me, pinning me down. "Don't," I say but the command carries no weight at all.

It amuses him and he grins. It is the first time I've seen him smile without the slightest hint of malice in his eyes. Now they gleam with challenge. He will follow through on his words. "Let me up," I demand.

"No," he replies. "Tonight is for me."

Alarm flashes like lightning down my spine. It is foolish to imagine Bastien to be anything but cruel. I struggle to free myself but he holds my wrists against the mattress and covers my mouth with his.

His kiss shocks the fight out of me. His lips pry mine open and his tongue thrusts against mine. I feel possessed, at his mercy—and yet he is not hurting me. Bastien silently commands my submission but that is not all he wants. "Kiss me back, damn you," he demands.

Surely I have imagined that. Surely that is not despair I see in his eyes. With a curse, he kisses me again. It steals my breath away. I feel his body tremble and this time I am sure it is not a ruse. I touch my tongue to his timidly and he stills. I blush. Did I do it wrong?

He gentles and the slide of his tongue against mine becomes more sensuous than demanding. I can meet him this way and I do. Bastien settles more fully over me and I gasp at the feel of his hard member against my hip.

"Now you fear," he whispers against my throbbing lips. He releases one of my hands to caress my cheek so gently. "Don't."

As though the gesture angered him, he snarls and shoves away from me. I am left baffled, wondering if he is going to leave me like this. Then my skirt lifts up and billows almost over my head. "What—"

"Don't move if you know what's good for you."

My drawers tear up the middle and his arms come around my thighs. He sets upon me with a growl, kissing the heated core of me the way he kissed my mouth. My body shoots through with tension and I arch off the mattress. With one hand he presses me back down. He is ravenous and shows no mercy. I am caught against his mouth as surely as if I were tied to him with the chains in his chambers and the things he does with his mouth, his tongue—his *teeth*—make me slap a hand over my mouth to muffle my cries.

Whatever he is doing, he does it more and I grit my teeth and hold my breath to keep quiet. I will not give him the satisfaction of hearing me scream. But how much longer can I hold out? He spears me with his tongue and my sex clenches around it. He groans and presses his mouth harder against me.

Pleasure explodes in my core, up my spine, and I cannot hold back my cry. My body is boneless and I feel his eyes on me, missing nothing as his clever hand strokes me and the pleasant waves of delight continue to rock through me.

I smile, even as drowsiness weighs my eyelids down. I've never felt so content before. I could be grateful to Bastien for showing me this. He said this night was for him but he gave me so much pleasure I cannot believe his intent was purely selfish.

Then, with a single sentence from those sinful lips of his, I fall headlong back into my sordid reality. "If only your precious Beast could see you now."

Chapter Fifteen

I refuse to watch Bastien walk away and leave me to my own devices. I do, however, hurry to put myself to rights, thinking he will continue his gloating in the company of my father and Amalia. Instead, I am told the lord has retired for the evening.

I dine with my family, determined to put the entire sordid episode behind me. I sip my wine, eat my food, and smile at the appropriate times. They are all empty gestures. I taste nothing, hear nothing. For all my strength of will I cannot make myself forget.

It is a torture I inflict on myself willingly, for I cannot myself understand how the evening took such a wretched turn. I knew Bastien's demands on me would eventually escalate. I suppose I simply did not expect them to do it quite so quickly. Yet despite the cruelty with which I have been abandoned, I have not been harmed. That is perhaps the most puzzling thing about it.

Bastien awakened me to something I never knew existed. He has taught me in one night the incredible pleasure to be found in a lover's arms; and the disquieting upheaval. It is a lesson I will never forget, and one I never intend to repeat. Yet I cannot say I regret it.

I do not notice the passage of time. Before I know it, dinner is finished and I excuse myself to retire to my room. The bed is still in shambles, evidence of my indiscretion. I could move to a different one but that would not erase the past. Strange, I can almost sense Bastien in the room even now. Of course, he would not return.

I lie down to sleep but I am not tired, my mind in too much turmoil to surrender to sleep.

Of all the things Bastien could have done he chose one meant to give pleasure without taking in return. He made me feel as though the world was coming apart at the seams and he was the only one holding it—and me—together. And I know he did not reach his own ends; the evidence of his passion was still there when he left me. Why would he do such a thing? Was his intent merely to humiliate me, show me that I am not so innocent?

I've no reason not to think the worst of him but I cannot believe that was his plan.

Perhaps…

Like the Beast, the man is a confusing contradiction. Now that I am alone, I can think and reason, and I can see what I have been too frightened to see even a month ago. Bastien can be cruel and cold. His words are vicious daggers meant to score the most painful of wounds and he is not at all hesitant to use them. Yet he has not harmed me or my family, though he's had plenty of opportunities.

He keeps reminding me we are nothing but his prisoners but he has treated us with the respect a man would show his honored guests. It was the Beast who gave us lodging, provided us with magnificent feasts, and anything our hearts desired. But three nights out of the month, the man honored those concessions and afforded us the privacy I asked of him. An unfeeling man would not have bothered to bargain. A cruel man would not have kept his word.

It occurs to me that I am the only one ever allowed to visit him on full moon nights. Not even the servants will dare enter his lair unless absolutely necessary. I can only imagine how he used to spend those nights before me. Chained? Utterly alone? Is it any wonder then that he acts like a caged animal?

I sit up in my cold bed as the gravity of this revelation sinks in. A caged animal—that is precisely what he reminds me of. A beast captured in the wild and locked away inside four walls, tethered by heavy chains, never to see the light of day. Bastien is so used to his solitary prison, being feared and hated, that even when a soul approaches in kindness he does not know how to react, except in anger. He takes his vengeance out on anyone who comes near, whether they deserve his wrath or not.

I understand now. Sympathy for this wretched creature melts away some of my bitterness. I have seen glimpses of a different side of him tonight. The look in his eyes, his words, at times so desperate; the way he caressed my cheek so carefully as if, at least for a moment, I was precious to him. He was not gentle but perhaps very briefly kind in his own way. I could almost believe there is a part of Bastien which longs to be good again; to break out of his prison and rejoin the world.

Yet even if that were true the other part of him, the near crazed, tortured and abandoned part holds him back. The part which madly fights for its freedom, willing to tear the world and itself apart just to see the sun rise bright and full again must regard any hint of kindness as a weakness.

How can I ever persuade him otherwise? It is a task almost too great for one woman to undertake. Not for the first time, hope mingles with helpless despair. I am almost certain there is good in Bastien. Coaxing it out of him, however, will not be easy. And if I am wrong, I might pay for my folly with my soul.

The day breaks in gloom and fog. Summer is turning to autumn and the country air is chill but a lovely fire burns in the library hearth, banishing the cold. The smell of books comforts me. No matter what life brings I can always seek sanctuary within their pages.

In no mood to converse with my family, I hide in a concealed nook with a soft lap blanket and a book of fairy tales. For a while, at least, I want to pretend that every obstacle can be overcome and deserving people truly can live happily ever after. Love can victor over all if it is strong and true enough.

"Whatever Bastien gives, it is only so he can take again." The Beast's glowing eyes look tired in the darkness of his hidden passageway. The cold tunnel stands open now, a grave breeze howling through it and stealing the warmth out of my bones. "I have warned you about him before."

There is gruff reproach in his growling voice which far overshadows the regret in his eyes. Though I have not fought Bastien's attentions last night, I did not invite them yet my Beast blames me for what happened? It angers me. "Yes, you have," I tell him. "You know what he is capable of, so why did you choose to come to my rooms yesterday mere moments before sunset?"

He must know everything that happened after his transformation otherwise he would not have said this. It shames me that his regard of me has lowered, but I will not bear the brunt of his indignation. I am not the only one at fault. He knows this, too, and hangs his leonine head. "I shouldn't have," he says. His paw shifts as though to come closer but he stays himself, remaining little more than a great shadow in his dark tunnel. "I just needed to see you before… I wanted to tell you good night."

Something Bastien did not do when he left me stunned in bed, with my clothes in shambles as much as my mind.

"What he did—"

"You did," I say.

He lifts his gaze to mine in surprise.

After all these months, all the patience I have shown him, all the roaring and threats I have endured, and the fate of everyone inside these walls weighing me down day after day, I cannot stand it any longer. It is too hard to try for so long and have so little to show for it. I am failing and I do not know how much longer I can keep fighting this losing war. It is exhausting and it infuriates me that after all that it somehow became my fault that Bastien took advantage of my moment of weakness.

"Both of you tell me you are not one and the same, and yet you remember everything. You know each other's minds. You know what the other is planning and you let it happen." The words come in a rush and with them a terrible realization. "You *let* it happen." Angry tears sting my eyes. I've given everything to this being; left myself at his mercy time and again. I've borne the Beast's torments, as I've shouldered Bastien's, hoping that my pleasance would better them in return.

And for all his now gentle words, I find that the fearsome, powerful Beast is a coward.

"It is all an excuse," I say, willing him to tell me otherwise; praying he can somehow explain himself. "Bastien is only as cruel as *you* allow him to be every time you choose to look the other way. You don't *want* to stop him... because it would mean admitting that he is part of you."

My Beast says nothing.

"He *is* part of you, even when you are like this, he's still with you, and you with him. Oh, God..." Two months of torment at Bastien's hands... and all the while they were the hands of the creature who swore to safeguard me. Bastien is the Beast? And the Beast is Bastien. Both of them are monstrous in different ways; both can and have hurt me unimaginably. Bastien is merely honest about it. "Say something, damn you."

The Beast's silence is his answer.

It is true, then; they are one and the same. Though one's form is different from the other, they never leave each other. That is how the Beast knows what Bastien does on the nights he is free, and how Bastien knows so much about me. They—are—*one*. "Can you influence each other?"

His gaze breaks away; he cannot even look at me. That means yes.

It means that everything Bastien has done, he could only have done if the Beast allowed it. "I trusted you." My voice is hardly a whisper but he can still hear.

He growls and turns away. "There's been no word of Marguerite," he says, retreating into the passageway. "I sent a messenger to look for her."

Then the bookcase slides back into place and it is as though he was never there. I stare down at the book of happy endings in my lap. It seems an alien thing that no longer belongs in my world. How could it? My world is ending as I sit here and nothing about it is in any way happy.

It is over.

I failed...

Chapter Sixteen

"Please, my lady, give him a chance." Aimee is on the verge of tears, desperate to keep me from leaving. She is not the only one. The household has been in a panic since I asked young Jocelyn to begin packing my belongings and alert my father and Amalia to our departure.

"I've given him months of chances, Aimee. I can't do it any longer. I am sorry. I cannot save Bastien. I don't think anyone can."

"But you're so close!"

"I've never been farther."

I will miss this castle but I cannot wait to put it behind me. The Beast knows what is afoot; he chooses not to intervene. It's for the better. We've said all there was to say, except perhaps good bye. Something tells me he will not stand on that final bit of formality.

I walk the grounds one last time bidding farewell to everyone I've come to know. Amalia is locked in her room; I can hear her crying from the staircase. She will blame me for this and I know I shall never hear the end of it. It would be of no use to try and talk to her when she is like this. Instead I go in search of my father.

I find him in the garden, sitting by the rose bush. He pats the seat next to him in invitation. "Amalia is deep in her theatrics, I gather."

I smile. "Yes. She threatened to kill herself."

Father chuckles. "Amalia has always had a passionate nature."

"And how are you?"

He sighs wearily. "I am... glad," he says. "A father wants only the best for his children. I hoped this would be the best for you. I was mistaken." He smiles and takes my hands in his. "Nothing could make me prouder of you, my child. You have a good heart, Lyssette. You always stand up for those who need it and fight for what you believe. But sometimes you must stand up for yourself. Hold on to that strength. There will be many times when you might need it still."

I don't feel strong. I feel a fool. Not once have I thought to seek answers beyond what the Beast told me. I trusted his word completely. I let my dreams and hopes blind me to the truth. A beast will always be a beast, no matter how hard one tries to change it.

Well, I know better now.

Our midday meal is a quiet, somber affair. Amalia sniffles on occasion, her face red from crying, but she is restraining herself to nothing more than scathing looks cast my way. The servants' reluctance to see us leave, and I suspect some trickery as well, makes packing drag on until sunset.

At the prospect of another night spent under this roof I nearly march out into the night on my own. For my safety, however, the hostler refuses to saddle a horse for me and I dare not pass through the forest on foot. I can hear wolves howling at the big, bright moon even now.

As I go in search of a quiet parlor to while away the evening until exhaustion claims me, the great door opens, admitting a scruffy young boy. He is winded and past him, on the drive, I see a horse being led away. This must be the messenger the Beast sent.

"You've news?"

He nods eagerly and pulls a crumpled letter out of his pocket. He smoothes it out before he hands it to me. "Thank you," I say. "Go to the kitchen to warm up, and tell Cook I said to feed you. You look starved."

He grins at me, his eyes shining. "Thank you, Mademoiselle!" And with a quick bow he scampers off.

"Good news, I hope." Jacques is composed as ever. Of all the servants he is the only one who did not plead with me to stay. I think he understands better than the rest why I cannot.

I open the letter, curious to see what my sister has written me.

At once I recognize that it is not Marguerite's hand. The letter is from Monsieur Lafarge. He writes:

A man of honor keeps his word. I have given mine to provide for Monsieur Clemens and his two daughters in the absence of the third. As Mademoiselle Marguerite now finds herself without the comfort and protection of her father's presence, it falls to me to secure her in a position befitting a young lady of her stature. I have asked for Marguerite's hand in marriage and she has happily accepted. The wedding will take place with all haste tomorrow morn and all are invited.

"My lady? Are you all right?"

I find myself leaning on Jacques, numb with shock. This must be a jest! Marguerite will marry Monsieur Lafarge? I cannot believe she would be so foolish; the man has twice her years and more. He's outlived two wives already and neither had given him the heir he'd so longed for.

"Mademoiselle... Lyssette. What can I do?"

God, Marguerite would not have agreed to this, would she? "Saddle two horses," I say, though I don't know how the words manage to make it past my lips.

"My lady, it would be wiser to wait until day break."

"Now!" I cannot risk waiting so long. It could be too late by the time I get there. If I am to save my sister from making the greatest mistake of her life, I need to leave immediately.

And I need help.

"Where is Bastien?"

Jacques draws himself up. "The lord is not receiving visitors tonight."

I extricate myself from his bracing hold and press the letter into his hands. "Take this to my father," I tell him and run up the staircase.

Jacques calls after me but I've neither the time nor the inclination to listen.

I do not even slow through the dark hallway, but rush right up to Bastien's door and push it open without knocking. He is on the bed, reading. "Get up," I say.

He raises an eyebrow at my rude entry; that is his only reaction. "You've come for more? I'm ever your humble servant." He inclines his head in a mocking bow. "Alas, it would seem our furry friend was not amused." With a sharp yank of his wrist, he makes the heavy chain binding him pull taut.

He is chained?

Panic wells inside my breast until I can hardly breathe. I look around frantically for the key but, of course, it will not be anywhere within reach. "Where is it?"

"Where is what?" There is amusement in his voice. He is enjoying this.

Footsteps thump on the floor behind me. Jacques catching up. "My lady, I really must insist!"

"Free him," I demand. "Lord Bastien and I are going for a horse ride."

"Why not a carriage?" he mocks.

"Horses are faster," I tell him.

"I cannot allow you to leave the castle grounds at night," Jacques insists.

"In a hurry, are we?" Bastien drawls.

"My sister is getting married tomorrow morning."

"Felicitations," he says dryly.

"To Jean Lafarge."

"Perhaps not, then."

"I need you to help me stop it," I say. It is impossible to stand still under that steady, unfeeling gaze, when my body hums with the need to move, to run. I know I have no chance at all of stopping the wedding on my own. Bastien, human as he is now, is my only hope. I cannot imagine what possessed Marguerite to make this devil's bargain. My heart tells me she is in danger and though we've had our differences in the past, she is my sister and I cannot let her come to harm.

"And why should I?" Bastien asks.

I have nothing to say. Nothing that would persuade him to take up my cause. I cannot appeal to his feelings or sense of honor—he has neither. And if he was not roused by the prospect of being freed from his chains, why should he care about leaving the castle?

"My lady, this is not the time to discuss these things."

I ignore Jacques' warning. "Please, Bastien." I am not too proud to beg. Or bargain. "I'll do anything."

His eyes briefly flare with lust and his entire body tenses. "No," he grates at last, turning back to his damned book.

Breath leaves me at that callous answer.

"And you will not be leaving the castle, either. Jacques, bar the gates and lock the door."

"You think to keep me from my sister?"

"The selfish meddlesome whore who took up with the first bastard who had coin enough to impress? Bloody yes, I'll keep you from her."

"I see," I return, "because I am clearly much better served keeping company with the heartless bastard who abused my trust, kept me prisoner, humiliated me and took advantage of me."

"You forgot clothed you, fed you, and provided you with all the books and frivolities you females hold so dear. You and your motley relatives. You should be grateful, Lyssette. I raised you far up from that hovel you called home. Your sister got precisely what she deserved. She and Lafarge should suit nicely together."

"I despise you."

He does not even bat an eyelash. "You are entitled."

Incensed beyond reason, I cannot keep my feet from moving forward. In three steps I am by his bed and my hand flies before I can stop it. I've never slapped a person before in my life. My palm throbs and his cheek reddens where I struck him. A muscle ticks in his jaw. His eyes burn with cold fury when he lifts his gaze to me again. "Stay here and rot, then," I tell him.

I turn on my heels, heading for the door.

"Lyssette," he calls after me.

I run out into the hall as chains rattle. "*Lyssette get back here!*" he roars. I cover my ears and refuse to listen. Servants stare at me as I rush past them. Heedless of everything, I run out to the stables. There is not time to saddle a horse. I choose a strong mare I am familiar with and mount her bareback. Her whinnies echo in the night as I urge her into a gallop toward the gate.

The path lays open before me. I squint into the darkness, trusting my mare to lead me true. She snorts and picks up her pace, as if she can sense my urgency, and as we fly through the night I whisper my soft good bye to a dream, bracing myself for the nightmare that is to come.

Chapter Seventeen

Clouds gather in an instant on a wicked faery wind, obscuring the night sky. I feel my mare tense and snort as lightning strikes in the distance but she stays her course, flying so fast through the woods I would think she wasn't moving at all, were it not for the beat of her hooves. Then we emerge onto the open fields and the sound is lost amidst the furious thunderclaps.

Lightning strikes a lone tree nearby. The mare rears and I grasp onto her mane to keep my seat. By sheer force of will I remain on her back and calm her enough to continue past the burning trunk toward my village. The driving rain stings my face and eyes; my hands are numb holding the reins. I do not let up.

Our cottage is near the edge of the village, just past the bridge now threatened by the swollen, churning waters of the creek. I race across it, heading toward the only home I've ever known. I hope and pray that I will find Marguerite there.

The cottage is dark. No candlelight flickers in the windows, no gentle puff of smoke rises up from the weathered chimney. My head knows what my heart refuses to accept: Marguerite would not be without a fire on a night like this. I dismount and push open the groaning door, shouting Marguerite's name even though I know she is not there. I call out again and again. I search around the cottage and in the small barn. It is empty, as it has been for years.

My dress is soaked through, the skirts tangling around my legs as I make my way back to the mare waiting trustingly where I left her. I am chilled to the bone but strangely the cold does not bother me. My shaking now has nothing to do with the icy rain and everything to do with my horrifying suspicion. I know where to find Marguerite.

"Please God let me be wrong," I pray, mounting the mare again. I slow my pace through the flooding village streets, dreading my destination. Water splashes up with each step my mare takes. The mud will loosen soon, making the going too treacherous to continue. I must make it to Marguerite before then.

Past the church square the streets widen. It is a straight road through the village to the hill where the Lafarge estate towers over everything, a majestic monarch watching over its subjects. Torches are burning on either side of the entrance, and every window of the house is aglow with light. No doubt there is a fire lit in every hearth but there is nothing warm about it.

I leave the mare untethered and pick up skirts weighted down with water to climb the marble staircase. The door before me is iron like a prison cage and the knocker is in the shape of a demonic gargoyle. Not even the Beast's lion head knocker had ever infused me with so much dread. I raise the heavy thing and let it drop. The ominous gong is underscored by thunder.

A flash of lightning turns the world briefly blue and when darkness returns, there is only the smoking torchlight to see by when the heavy door slowly opens.

"Lyssette," Monsieur Lafarge says in greeting, his sickly wrinkled face creasing into a semblance of a smile. He is nearly of a height with me, his weathered body disguised with expensive clothes. His hair has been white for as long as I have known him and in his advanced age it is thinning, making him appear even more skeletal. "I rather hoped to see you again."

"I received your message," I tell him, grateful that my teeth stopped chattering long enough for me to speak clearly.

"Did you? Then you've come to offer your congratulations? I humbly accept."

"I've come to take my sister home."

His laugh is more of a cough. "Fanciful child. What do you imagine she will say to that?"

"Whatever is on her mind, she will say it to me directly."

I put all my weight against that door to open it fully. He has no choice but to allow it, weak as he is. I care nothing for the frailty of his age. "I want to see her now," I say coming inside. It is terribly rude to barge into someone's home uninvited. Then again, so is coercing one's sister into an ill suited marriage.

"Of course," Lafarge says. "I live but to serve." A devil's words. The door closes behind me with a resounding gong like a massive church bell. "I believe your sister is in the back parlor."

I take that as an invitation to find my own way. The halls I pass through are filled with portraits looking down on me. The Lafarge mansion is not one tenth the size of the Beast's castle, yet the maze-like passages make it seem endless. I call out Marguerite's name again and again, getting more worried each time she does not respond.

"Marguerite, answer me! Where are you?"

At last I hear her reedy voice and hasten my footsteps to the parlor at the end of the hall. Only the hearth fire burns low to illuminate the room. My sister sits primly in a rocking chair which does not move. She is composed and dressed in a lovely violet gown but her hair is loose, falling in unruly waves to her waist and hiding one side of her face.

"Why are you here?" she asks in a brittle voice.

I draw nearer. "I received word that you are to be married. I had to see for myself."

"You've seen me. It is true." She smiles cruelly. "I'm to be married to a man of means. You can go back to your monster."

"Is this truly what you want?" It cannot be. Everything about this place, about Lafarge and my sister is wrong. I don't know what it is, but dread ties my insides into knots.

"It is," Marguerite says. "I want you to leave. You are not welcome in this house."

"Marguerite, I—"

"Go!" she shouts and her eyes glitter as her hands curl into fists in her lap. More softly, she adds, "For God's sake, Lyssette, get out of here."

I rush to her and take her face in my hands. She flinches and I brush her hair aside, gasping at the sight her face presents. Her eye is swollen nearly shut and a dark bruise mars her features from her temple to her chin. "My God, Marguerite. Who did this to you?"

Marguerite's tears spill down her cheeks. "It's you he wants," she whispers.

I do not waste time. Taking her hand, I pull her to her feet. "We're leaving. Now." Lafarge has not yet caught up to me. There is no telling what he is planning but I don't intend to be here when he gets around to it.

The parlor, more of a gentleman's smoking room, has no other door except the one I entered through. There are swords crossed above the hearth, too far for me to reach, but a pair of pistols gleams in an intricate case on the mantle. I know nothing of weapons; not even how to check if it is loaded. The weight of it in my hand comforts me, as it frightens me.

I lead the way out into the hall but cannot remember the way I came. I turn corner after corner, try every door I come to. The ones which are unlocked open onto more rooms with no other way out. Lafarge's laughter echoes all around; it is impossible to tell where the sound is coming from. He is mocking us and Marguerite is already weeping with fright.

Just as I am about to lose hope, I open a door and see the garden through the windows. We will have to climb through them. I thank God they are low enough to the ground to do it. I help Marguerite through as quietly as possible and follow her outside.

The lightning has abated but the rain is still strong.

"Lyssette!" Lafarge's furious roar is much louder than should be possible from a man of his constitution.

Marguerite cries out, her fingers digging painfully into my arm. "Lyssette, let's go!"

But where? I look around and see nothing familiar. No one I know has ever come this far east of the village. Beyond the baker's house, the land belongs to Lafarge and he is insistent upon his privacy. Now I can see why. Beyond the fields which make all farmers jealous, the land is dead and barren. The ground will not drink of the rain water and so it pools and floods.

There is nowhere to hide and too far to run for shelter. It would be too far to run to get out of sight; Lafarge would see us. "Stay behind me, Marguerite."

"No," she cries, pulling me away. "We need leave. We can outrun him!"

Perhaps, but where would we go? Where would he not find us?

"*Lyssette!*"

Marguerite screams. Lafarge is coming around from a side balcony and he has a musket in hand.

"You won't get away from me again, Lyssette!"

Shock makes my arms numb and I nearly drop the pistol. It takes strength I do not feel to raise it. I pull back the flint lock, my hand shaking. "Stay back!"

"You belong to me!"

I close my eyes and pull the trigger. Nothing happens. My heart sinks. The pistol isn't loaded.

Lafarge raises the musket to his shoulder. "You'll stay here one way or another!"

Marguerite screams and runs. I pray she finds shelter; my own feet are rooted to the spot. Fear grips me and I cannot move, not even to duck for cover. The rain eases and I think I hear hoof beats. It is nothing but the hammering of my own heart.

"You abandoned me!"

I hear someone scream my name and my vision clears to take in more of what surrounds me, though I cannot believe what I am seeing. A dark rider approaches at a furious pace, a sword gleaming in his hand. Lafarge doesn't see him. His arms shake as he levels his musket at me. The ground shakes at the rider's approach; he is upon us.

His gleaming blade slashes down and Lafarge cries out. The musket drops from his grasp as the rider dismounts at full gallop, taking a stand between me and the weathered demon. Past his massive shoulders rising with each breath, I see Lafarge on the ground, his eyes wide as an owl. "Demon!" he screams.

My rescuer says not a word, though his hold on the sword tightens.

"Please," I hear myself saying.

He tenses. "I should have killed you all those years ago," he snarls and my legs nearly give way. Bastien? Impossible.

"It can't be you!" Lafarge says. "My God… you haven't aged a day…"

"And now you'd dare take what's mine?"

"I… she belongs to me!"

Bastien rushes the old man.

"No!" I cry and to my shock, he stops. "Please, just take me away from here."

He turns to me, his face a mask of fury. "I told you not to leave my castle," he growls.

"Is that why you're here? Because I disobeyed you?"

"You should have listened! You knew how mad he is and still you threw yourself right into his arms!"

Behind him I see movement. Lafarge! "Bastien!" I shout.

He dives for me. His arms squeeze me so tight it hurts and his body bows over me, shielding me completely. A shot from the musket deafens me. I feel the impact; hear Bastien's breath explode from his chest. He holds me tight while my ears continue to ring.

Bastien's groan of pain terrifies me. He shudders against me and his hold loosens. I am able to stand and turn to see him stagger away from me. Sword still in hand, he turns on Lafarge and stalks him on unsteady legs. Lightning strikes, illuminating his bloodied back. I hold back my cry, knowing instinctively that he cannot last much longer.

Lafarge scrambles back in retreat. He slips in the gathering mud and his moans of terror make me shake with fear. But I fear for Bastien more. Once again, the man I thought a monster raises his sword and brings it down on Lafarge, silencing his bleating cries.

Bastien releases the sword and stumbles back, turning unsteadily to face me. Tears blur my vision as I go to him. He breathes my name as his eyelids droop, and then he falls to his knees and collapses on the ground.

My own scream echoes across the night.

Chapter Eighteen

I drop to my knees next to him and cradle his head in my lap. The rain is abating now and by the light of the full moon I see his lips are deathly pale and the ground around us is soaking with his blood.

He is shaking, eyes closed against the softly falling rain. I lean over him to shield him. "Oh, God, Bastien… I'm so sorry. This is all my fault."

A small smile pulls on his mouth. "No. It was always meant to end this way."

"W-what?"

Behind me Marguerite sobs. When she returned I cannot tell. All my attention is on Bastien. He coughs, a horrible sound. "One dies," he says, "for the other to be free."

"No!" I cry. "This is mad. Why should anyone have to die?"

"Part of… curse."

I refuse to accept that. "Marguerite run. Take the mare, ride to the healer's house. I don't care what you must do but get him here."

Wide eyed, she nods and runs.

"Too late," Bastien says, his teeth chattering. "Getting cold."

I lean over him more and rub his arms. "Of course you are. It's freezing out here. That doesn't mean you're going to die." I look around for something, anything, that will help me keep him warm. There is nothing. My cloak lays heavy and sodden over my shoulders. It would only cool him more. It is too far to the house, I cannot get him inside on my own.

He opens his eyes just a little. "I could almost believe you care for me."

"Of course I care." God, where is Marguerite?

"Maybe that's enough. To keep me out of hell."

"Stop it this instant! No more talk of death or hell. Marguerite will be back with the healer soon, you'll see. And then you'll feel very foolish for being so dramatic."

He smiles again, one hand reaching up to brush my cheek. But he is too weak already to do it. I take his hand and press it to my cheek. It is cold as ice.

Bastien's smile fades and his eyelids droop as the night fall silent. There is no more rain and the air is still as death. The starry sky above us steals what little warmth remains.

"Bastien?" I shake him. "Bastien!"

He gasps in a deep breath. His body expands, changes, grows. I've never seen magic like this. Where before his transformations have been harsh and painful, the one I am witnessing now is anything but. He changes smoothly, a thing not physical but transcendent. I can feel Bastien fading away until all that remains is the Beast. The weight of him is crushing but I dare not move or breathe.

I count my heartbeats, waiting for him to stir. One died. Would the other live? Would he want to? Bastien is gone forever. There will be no more full moon nights; no respite to humanity from his beastly form. Beast will never again be able to walk among people. The curse is broken, but not the way either of us wished it.

He rouses his brows drawing in a frown before he opens his eyes and blinks up at me. "Lyssette?"

I swallow back my grief. He is alive. I attempt a smile, though my sight blurs with tears. "H-how do you feel?"

The great beast groans and raises his head from my lap. He sits up and twists to kneel before me. He appears to be fully healed. But of course he would. Beast is not the one who was wounded. For the first time I can truly believe that they are… *were* not one and the same.

"I…" he paws at his shoulder and chest. There is no more wound to be found. I wait for his great sigh of relief but instead his shoulders sink as his eyes fill with despair. "Oh, Lyssette."

"You're alive," I tell him. "The curse is broken."

"I never wanted this," he murmurs, unable to meet my gaze.

"You're alive," I tell him again, more strongly. "Nothing else matters."

Beast cups my cheek gently, his fur rasping over my skin. "Of course it does," he says. "The curse may have split me into two but my heart was always one and the same." His great paw lowers. "We both loved you equally, though Bastien would never have said so. He would have made you the husband I never can. *Of course that matters.*"

My throat aches. I want to scream to the heavens, demand they right this wrong. I can't bear to see my Beast suffer anymore. He's held out hope for so long, and even in his moment of victory all happiness is stolen from him. He has nothing now.

No, that is a lie. He has me. "I swore to you I would never leave," I tell him. "And I will stand by my word. No matter what."

He sighs. "You will leave, Lyssette. You must. I deserved my curse, you did not. I…" He looks away. "I don't want you coming back to the castle."

I am rendered speechless by his words.

A chill wind makes me shiver. Beast rises to his full height, towering over me, and offers his paw. "You need to get inside. You're freezing out here." So was he a few moments ago. It is the most difficult thing I've ever had to do to raise my hand to his, mirroring his nonchalance. He helps me to my feet and I lean on him far more than I wish to while I regain my balance.

The wind tugs at my gown and hair. My teeth chatter and I cannot stop shaking. I will catch my death out here soon. But I cannot make myself draw nearer to Beast's warmth for I know that I will never be able to let go again.

Whilst I still can, I step back from him. I am weary, swaying on my feet. He reaches out to steady me but I hold my hand up to stay him. Pain flashes in his eyes. No more than I've felt for months.

In my exhaustion I imagine the world around me is changing. But when I look about, I see it is not my imagination. The wind doesn't howl anymore as it did before; it whispers. Countless voices fly on a rush of air, their words hushed with secrecy and intrigue. I hear Bastien among them. I hear the Beast.

I hear a woman's laughter and a voice so ethereal it banishes the cold of the night.

He hears them too. His eyes dart around, seeking the source.

The earth steams as it warms but I still shiver in my wet gown. There is light to see by, though it is still full night, the dawn hours away. Where is it coming from?

"Have you learned your lesson, lover?" that diaphanous voice hisses. The question echoes, rushing past us, between us; around us. I feel the Beast's animosity. His snarl is vicious and bloodthirsty. "Has dying cured your apathy?"

More voices, laughter and cruel shouts which despite their malevolence still sound sweet as a lullaby. What are these creatures? The ground warms beneath my feet and miniscule blades of grass sprout around us.

"Lilith," Beast growls.

The creature laughs, the sound so beautiful it pains my ears. Light blinds me and I shield my eyes against its glare. When it dims and night returns I blink at the female standing before me. She is tall and lithe, draped in silken robes which move like ocean waves. Her hair is like spun gold, glittering about her beautiful face and her eyes shimmer like stars, just as distant—just as cold. "Lover," she purrs to my Beast. "It's been so long. Three hundred years since the night you abandoned me. Do you regret it now, human? Do you wish you stayed in my... good graces?" She smoothes her hand down her breast and the silken dress becomes translucent.

Beast growls, baring his fangs. "You narcissistic bitch!"

The female clucks her tongue in censure. "Oh, now, that is a lovely bit of hypocrisy coming from you, Bastien. I remember how you loved those mirrors in my bower. I thought you wished to see me. But it was yourself you were so enamored with."

He growls again. "I was a fool to ever think of you as a conquest."

She smiles. "Yes, a fool to think you could ever win me."

"A blind fool, seeing beauty in an empty shell," he snaps.

She hisses.

Beast bares his teeth again, crouching low.

"Ah-ah," Lilith warns coldly. "I know what you're thinking. And I would not advise it. You might not care for *your* life any longer but there is another you hold dear." She circles me and I am frozen, unable to move or even blink.

Roses bloom at my feet, long vines with sharp thorns winding upward around my legs. I feel them scraping my flesh. A single move will cause them to pierce my skin and I somehow know those barbs are poisonous. I dare not even breathe.

"Damn you, Lilith! Release her!"

Lilith laughs and tears leak from my eyes. "You're in no position to make demands on me, Bastien," she says. "After all your trespasses you should show some respect. Perhaps some groveling would not be amiss."

Beast's gaze meets mine briefly, fear sparking in their depths, but it is replaced by rage as he once again looks upon the inhumanly beautiful Lilith. "What do you want?"

Her smile is sharp as a blade. "Oh, my dear, beautiful monster. I want what every woman wants. *Everything.*"

Beast's eyes narrow on her. "You want me."

A blood red rose bends toward her and Lilith caresses its petals, playing coy. She answers Beast with a shrug of one delicate shoulder and the air shimmers between us, shadows taking shape. I watch wide eyed as a scene unfolds, countless reflections mirroring a pair of bodies as they writhe among silken sheets. Moans of pleasure answer passionate sighs. They are echoed by the many voices around us. The world breathes in the rhythm of their loveplay, infusing the air with agonizing lust.

"We were beautiful together, you and I," Lilith says, her voice dreamy with remembrance.

I breathe in and my body tenses with cruel longing. With every moment that stretches on, the pain of unrequited desire intensifies until I want to scream. I am denied.

"You were everything a lover should be and more. Fearless. Dauntless. You used to feed on my pleasure, as I fed on yours."

My eyes sting with tears. I want to shake my head but I cannot move; I can't even close my eyes to escape the scene. It is not love, or even sex. It is torture. The sighs turn pleading, the moans become cries of pain. The world breathes faster, a broken rhythm of gasps as though some great being is about to expire beneath my feet. I blink and red hazes my vision, minuscule drops of blood spiking my lashes. The pain behind this driving need is unbearable. I feel as though I am the one in this vision, dying in a futile attempt to achieve something forever beyond my grasp.

"I would have given you everything," Lilith says. "Beauty and riches, delicacies such as you've never tasted and revelries you never could have imagined. I would have made you immortal, lover. And you spat in my face."

I tear my gaze away from the scene to seek my Beast. Our eyes meet, his filled with shame and regret, mine with sorrow and helpless despair. I see no way out of this predicament. Lilith is a creature unlike any I have ever seen or read about. She is powerful in ways I can hardly comprehend, and she wants something I have no way of denying her.

My heart bleeds for the Beast. He whines low, shifting closer as if he wants to come to me, but the briars coiled around me pull taut, sharp thorns tearing into my gown. I gasp and he stops.

"You love this creature," Lilith says to me, a questioning lilt to her voice. "Do you love him despite his monstrous form?"

My throat works and I struggle to answer, "Yes."

"Do you love him despite the cruelty of his human side?"

"Yes," I say, to my Beast this time.

She leans so close her lips brush the whorls of my ear as she whispers, "Will you still love him when he is mine?"

I have never known a feeling like this. It blooms in my chest and fills me from the top of my head to the tips of my toes, banishing the ache and sorrow of Bastien's past. That is all it is: the past. The beautiful prince turned monster has had three hundred years to regret his mistake, and I can see in his eyes now that he is no longer the man Lilith imagines him to be, if he ever was to begin with.

I see the man he has become. One who, instead of saving himself, sacrificed his own life to protect mine; who, even at his worst, has shown himself capable of great kindness and generosity.

"He will never be yours," I say and the surety of it gives me strength enough to meet Lilith's shining gaze without flinching.

She smiles. "We will see." She glides across her own contrived vision to Beast.

He launches at her with a fearsome snarl, but her form is momentarily no more tangible than mist and he falls through it to the other side.

Lilith remains unharmed.

Her laughter makes the voices keen as Beast claws at my rosethorn prison with a fervor borne of desperation. The briars tear into his paws. Where a vine snaps, another replaces it. Where a bloom drops to the ground, a new branch sprouts and coils upward, lashing at him.

Lilith laughs at his attempts.

"Stop," I say. "Please. It's no use."

Breathing hard, he pauses long enough to see his bloodied paws. His eyes meet mine again, helpless, hopeless.

"You can't free me."

He drops heavily to all fours, his great mane brushing against my cheek. "Forgive me."

"You understand now, don't you?" Lilith says.

He nods and seems to lack the strength to raise his head. "Yes."

"What?" I ask, a terrible dread making my body quiver.

"She will not release you until she has what she wants."

"No... *No!* You can't!"

"I must," he says.

"He will," Lilith echoes.

"Why?" I demand brokenly.

"Because he doesn't belong in this world anymore. From the moment he stepped into my bower, he was mine, and deep down, he's always known it."

Beast looks at me, his mouth twisting into a bitter little smile. "Because I love you."

"No, no, no…"

"I will go with you," he says to Lilith, humbled. Defeated.

"No, please!" I writhe in my prison, heedless of the poisonous barbs cutting into me, branding me with their searing venom.

Beast steps between us, facing his ageless foe. He kneels, as best he can in his fearsome form, and bows his head. "I will be yours. If you free her."

His words hold magic. They shimmer in the air and make it difficult to draw breath. He speaks them with such finality the fight leeches out of me. I sag and my prison releases me to drop to my knees.

Lilith smiles. She glides forward to claim her prize, and I cannot stand to see her touch him. I struggle to my feet, desperate to get to him, but before she reaches my Beast, Lilith stops. I watch the smile fade from her lips. She tries again, and strikes some invisible barrier in front of her. Anger makes her glow even brighter as she hurls herself forward again and again, each hit like the gong of a soundless bell. It shudders through the air, the ground beneath my feet. My head throbs with it and I am rendered deaf to the world at large.

Slowly, a heavy magic settles over us and I look up to watch Lilith's face transform with comprehension. Shock turns to denial, then anger, and then she screams her rage to the sky as jagged lightning bolts strike down in a mad storm around her, charring the earth and filling the air with thick black smoke.

I fall to the ground, curled into a ball to shield myself from her maelstrom as best I can. I want to reach out to my Beast, call to him, but I've lost all sense of direction.

Then, suddenly, it stops and everything grows quiet. I chance opening my eyes. The air is crisp and clean, the sky glittering with countless stars.

I look for Lilith, but she isn't there.

I seek my Beast next, but he is gone as well.

In his place, Bastien lays on the cold, hard ground, eyes closed as though in death. My desperate cry pierces the silence. I rush to him, not caring that my own wounds are healed, ignoring the galloping approach of Marguerite and the healer. I pull my beloved into my arms and pray he is still alive.

He is so cold, so very still.

"Live," I demand. "*Live, damn you!*"

I sense Marguerite and the healer with me, but choose not to see. They speak to me, but I refuse to hear their words. My heart, my soul, and all that I have left to give is focused solely on the man in my arms.

"You died for me once," I tell him. "A coward's way out. I want you to live. For me—for *us*." My voice breaks.

The healer grasps my arm to pull me away. I won't let him. "Mademoiselle, it's no use."

"He's gone, Lyssette," Marguerite says with such earnest sorrow I almost believe she's right.

"No." I refuse to accept that. "He can't die. I won't let him."

"Mademoiselle, please!"

I shove the healer off me. "Wake up, Bastien. Wake up!" I slap his face, beat at his chest. My hands are numb, and my face wet with more useless tears. What good are they now? What good is any of it? "*Live!*" I scream, shaking Bastien with all the strength I have left.

His lips part on a sigh so small I think I imagined it.

I stop and hold my breath, quietly praying for absolution—his and mine. My heart aches with desperate hope. "Bastien?"

I lay my hand on his chest to better feel its rise and fall. There, another breath! And his heartbeat, weak, fluttering against my palm. His brows pull into a frown, lips moving to form soundless words. I lean in close to hear, "My... strength."

Epilogue

Winter comes early. I sit in the library and watch flakes of snow waft down. They melt as soon as they touch the ground, but they are only portents of many cold, bitter months to come.

I don't mind. I have a beautiful castle to call home, my family all safely under one roof, and a cherished lover to secretly keep me warm when the nights grow cold.

Smiling to myself, I go in search of my prince.

He is not in the east wing atelier where he usually goes to paint in the afternoons. Frowning, I guess at his whereabouts and turn my feet toward the west wing. Neither of us have stepped foot in it this last month, not since the night Lilith burst back into this world and just as quickly disappeared.

I am happy to be rid of her, but Bastien is still uneasy. Worry shadows his blue eyes more and more as the weeks go by. I know what he fears. The moon will rise full tonight and neither of us knows what dark magic it will bring.

It pains me to see him so tormented. I want to comfort him, but don't know how.

He's asked me to be his wife, and I happily agreed, eager to bind myself to him straight away so he might see there is nothing to fear, that I will always stand by his side, no matter what. But, though Bastien was overjoyed to hear it, he refused to make any plans for a wedding until this full moon passes.

The west wing is being repaired. Rooms are aired out, portraits and paintings restored to their proper place. Bastien's bed chambers will be furnished again, but will no longer house the master of this castle. Too many bad memories have soaked into it, too many nightmares and too much pain. They linger like shadows in the anteroom, more of them in the main chamber where I now find my beloved.

The chains which once used to bind him are clutched in his hands. They should have been torn out of the wall weeks ago. "I thought I might find you here," I say softly.

Bastien looks at me and smiles a little. His fears in no way banished by my presence alone, they are at the very least lessened, and the oppressive silence lifts when he speaks my name in greeting. He says it now with such love and reverence it makes my heart flutter every time. When he beckons, I go to him, savoring the way he pulls me close and presses a kiss to my temple.

"What are you doing in here?" I ask.

He sighs heavily. "Preparing."

"But you said yourself there is probably nothing to worry about, that you haven't felt the Beast inside you since Lilith."

"I did," he says. "But after so long... it's difficult to believe it myself."

I trace the thick links of one chain. "I don't like seeing you with these."

Bastien chuckles. "I've worn them for three centuries. I've hated them so much I learned to love them in the end. The prison they represent is part of me now. The chains are nothing more than a symbol of it."

"Still. Put them away. Let's leave here. I want us to dine with my family tonight. I promise you, nothing bad will happen."

"I can't. You go ahead. Give them my apologies."

I huff with impatience. "I am not leaving you here alone."

Bastien scowls at me.

I refuse to be moved. "If you stay here, then I stay as well."

"If the chains don't hold—"

"They've held for three hundred years. And anyway, you won't need them." To convince him of my trust, I take the heavy chains from him and drag them back into the corner where they belong. Dusting my hands off, I nod to him and cross my arms. "There."

Bastien stares me with a very strange look in his eyes. He doesn't say a word.

I go to him at once and bring his hand up to my cheek. "You won't hurt me," I tell him.

But nothing I do or say can persuade him to leave the chamber for the rest of the day. I ring for Jacques to bring our dinner and tell him to let everyone know what might happen. I expect him to have the same faith in his master I do, to tell him there is nothing to be afraid of, but the loyal butler merely meets Bastien's gaze and they nod to each other and it occurs to me they've done this before.

I cannot imagine how Bastien must have felt during his first full moon, but the look on Jacques' face tells me it must have been terrible.

I stop arguing.

Whatever we are about to face, I know we will face it together, but I will let it be on Bastien's terms. I let the servants remove all the furniture, even the bed and, though it pains me, I help make a nest for Bastien on the floor so he can be comfortable. I sit with him through an early dinner and when he asks me to help him with the chains, I square my resolve and lock the shackles around his wrists.

I read aloud from book after book of happy endings. It must annoy him; Bastien prefers his tales to be filled with adventure and fearless warriors, not swooning heroines and flawless princes, but he never says a word in complaint. I scarcely think he hears anything beyond the sound of my voice. Nevertheless, I keep reading. It is as much for my comfort as it is his.

But I grow tired of hearing myself speak and, as the sun begins to set, the words I read become so monotonous I begin to fade. Somehow, despite my determination to stand steadfast by my prince, I fall asleep.

I startle awake to a strange sound. Full night has fallen and the hearth fire is burning so low I can see little more than shadows in the room. Across from me, Bastien sits on the nest of blankets and pillows I made for him, still blessedly human, and staring at something in his hand.

"Bastien?"

He looks up and I gasp at the glitter of tears in his eyes.

"What's happened?" I go to him, stumbling over the tangle of my skirts. His shackles are gone, the chains missing and the wall whole, as if it had never moored them at all. I cup Bastien's hands in mine and turn my body to raise them to the fire's dying light.

In one, he holds a dark red rose, fragrant in full, heavy bloom though none of our roses have flowered in weeks.

In the other is a strange, hand painted tarot card. On its face is a humble cottage, and in front of it a couple locked in an embrace so tight their bodies meld together at their feet and form the trunk and roots of a mighty oak. The card reads, *The Lovers*.

"I don't understand."

Bastien chuckles, a sound of astonishment rather than mirth. "*Find someone to love, or stay this way forever.* Lilith's own words defeated her. She could not touch me because her spell is broken. She is truly gone. And not because I died but… because I love you." He laughs and joy fills my heart. "I love you!"

When he crushes me into his arms, I go willingly. When he buries his face against my neck and laughing sobs shudder through his frame, I embrace my prince and smile through tears of my own.

His joyous shout summons the guard from the hallway. Taking one look at the two of us, the man whoops with glee and runs out, calling for the others.

I laugh wetly. He will wake the entire castle and I am glad for it. I want everyone to know the curse is finally broken.

At long last, it is over.

We are free.

The End

About the Author

ALIANNE DONNELLY is an avid lover of stories of all kinds. Having grown up with fairy tales in a place where it almost seemed they were real, it was no surprise when she began making up her own stories. She loves books, hiking, archery, and won't shy away from travel and zip lining. Alianne graduated with a business degree and when she's not off in the land of fantasy, she lives in California.

To find out more about Alianne's books and works in progress, visit her website at AlianneDonnelly.com.

Made in the USA
Charleston, SC
17 December 2013